After

Fire

BECKY CITRA

ORCA BOOK PUBLISHERS

Library and Archives Canada Cataloguing in Publication

Citra, Becky
After the fire / written by Becky Citra.

ISBN 978-1-55469-246-0

I. Title.

PS8555.I87A64 2010   jC813'.54   C2009-906859-1

First published in the United States, 2010
Library of Congress Control Number: 2009940905

Summary: When Melissa spends the summer at a wilderness lake with her single-parent mother and bratty younger brother, she makes friends with Alice, a mysterious girl with a strange fantasy life.

Orca Book Publishers gratefully acknowledges the support for its publishing programs provided by the following agencies: the Government of Canada through the Canada Book Fund and the Canada Council for the Arts, and the Province of British Columbia through the BC Arts Council and the Book Publishing Tax Credit.

Cover design by Teresa Bubela
Text design and typesetting by Nadja Penaluna
Cover photography by Getty Images

ORCA BOOK PUBLISHERS
PO Box 5626, STN. B
VICTORIA, BC CANADA
V8R 6S4

ORCA BOOK PUBLISHERS
PO Box 468
CUSTER, WA USA
98240-0468

www.orcabook.com
Printed and bound in Canada.
Printed on 100% PCW recycled paper.
13 12 11 10 • 4 3 2 1

For my mother, who taught me to love books

One

Melissa filled her garbage bag with half-dried clothes, heaved it over her shoulder and left the Laundromat. She glanced up and down the sidewalk, hoping that none of the kids from school would see her. She was positive they all had washing machines and dryers in their houses.

She checked to make sure the brochure was still tucked into the back pocket of her jeans. What were the chances of Mom saying yes? Her heart thudded. Why shouldn't she be allowed to go? Mom was working full-time now and she had hinted, *hinted*, that Melissa might be able to do something fun this summer.

The apartment building where she lived with her mother and her little brother Cody was eight blocks away if she followed the main street but a little bit shorter if she cut down the alley behind the 7-Eleven. Melissa didn't like going that way because there were always a couple of creepy-looking teenagers hanging around the Dumpster. She was sure they were doing some kind of drugs—they weren't always the same kids but they looked the same, with their white faces, blank eyes and black hoodies.

It was such a hot day that she decided to take the shortcut anyway. The garbage bag of damp clothes was already making her shoulder ache. To her relief the alley was empty, and she hurried as the apartment building came into sight.

The sign at the front of the building was missing letters, so instead of saying *Skyline Garden Apartments*, it said *Sk l e Gard n Apartm ts*. The word *Garden* was a joke, unless you counted the pots of geraniums on the balcony of their neighbor, a single woman named Dana who complained a lot about Cody's noise. Melissa climbed the stairs to the third floor and lugged the garbage bag to the door at the end of the hall. She could hear music and, when she opened the door, her mother's loud throaty laugh.

Perfect timing. Mom sounded like she was in a good mood, and Cody was at a birthday party. Melissa left the clothes in the narrow hallway, stepped over one of Cody's trucks and went into the tiny kitchen.

Her mother, Sharlene, and her friend, Jill, were sitting at the kitchen table drinking coffee. Sharlene's blond hair was tied up in a ponytail. Her long legs, in tight blue jeans, were stretched out in front of her, and she was wearing an aqua halter top. Beside her, Jill looked very plain in a white blouse and beige pants. Her mother had a way of doing that to people, Melissa had noticed. Everyone was always surprised when they found out that Melissa, who had dull brown hair and a sturdy build, was Sharlene's daughter.

"Hi, darling," said Sharlene. She was holding a cigarette, which she set down in a saucer. "You're an angel. Was it horrible?"

"It was okay," said Melissa. "But I didn't have enough money, so the clothes aren't dry."

"Hi, Melissa," said Jill.

"Hi," said Melissa.

Melissa was never quite sure what to call Jill. At school she was Mrs. Templeton. She taught the fourth-grade class across the hall from Melissa's grade-six classroom. But lately she spent so much time at their apartment, she had told Melissa to call her Jill when they weren't at school. There was no way Melissa could do that. Mrs. Templeton had been Melissa's teacher in grade four, long before she had become her mother's best friend. So Melissa solved the problem by not calling her anything.

3

There was one thing Melissa just didn't get. Why would Mrs. Templeton *choose* to be friends with someone like her mother? Mrs. Templeton was very nice and very ordinary. She could have been best friends with anyone.

Just after Christmas, Sharlene had been laid off from her job waitressing at Smitty's. She had spent weeks trying to find something else. Her smoking increased from six cigarettes a day to a pack and a half, and Melissa was terrified that her mother was going to get cancer. Cody had started wetting his bed again, and Melissa had to sign up at the school office for the free lunch program, which was humiliating.

And then Sharlene greeted her one day after school with a huge smile. "I've got a job, honey! Finally!"

Melissa was relieved until she found out what it was. "The custodian? You're going to be the new custodian at *my* school?"

"It's temporary," said Sharlene. "I'm taking over while Mr. Shore is away on sick leave. But I have a feeling it could lead to something permanent. The word is that the poor man is not doing all that well."

"You can't!" Melissa had said instantly. School was hard enough. She didn't fit in, even though she had been going to Huntley Elementary since grade three. All through grade three and most of grade four, Melissa had been invisible. She was shy at school, and she had never dared to invite kids home. After that terrible night two years ago, people started noticing her. But now they felt sorry for her, which wasn't the same as liking her.

Her mother, the custodian? She'd be there, sweeping the hallways, every day. This was way, *way* worse than getting a free lunch. But three months later, Melissa had to admit it had turned out okay. Sharlene actually liked the job and was thrilled when Mr. Shore decided not to come back. Cody, whose day care was in a portable behind the school, was ecstatic because he got to see Sharlene every day at lunchtime. He'd had two months of dry nights.

To Melissa's amazement, her mother was popular. Mr. Shore used to leave nasty messages on the blackboard about the students' messy desks. Sharlene never did that. The teachers joked around with her, and Mrs. Templeton, whom Melissa had always liked a lot, became her mother's new best friend.

Melissa picked up a cookie from a plate on the table. Then she put the cookie down. She had planned to introduce the idea casually, but before she could stop herself she blurted, "Mom! They had this brochure at school. There's an art camp in Kelowna in July! It's at the university. There's going to be pottery and painting and sculpture and…" Melissa produced the brochure and flapped it in the air. Her hands were shaking. "There's even going to be silver casting and you can make jewelry!"

"Let me see," said Sharlene calmly.

Melissa chewed her lip while her mother scanned the brochure. Sharlene's eyebrows shot up in the air. "It's six hundred dollars, sweetie!"

"It includes your room and all your meals," said Melissa desperately.

"I should think so! But six hundred dollars. That's almost a month's rent!"

"You said we were saving money now."

"Exactly. Saving. I'm not going to blow it all on some art camp!"

"Mom, *please*."

"No, Melissa. Forget it."

The back of Melissa's eyes burned. When she had first read the brochure at lunchtime on Friday, the idea of staying at a university with a bunch of kids she didn't know had been scary. But the thought of all that art made her feel dizzy with longing. She had stayed awake for hours the night before thinking about it, planning how to approach Sharlene. Now that she had asked, she felt like she would die if she didn't get to go.

Sharlene took a long drag on her cigarette. "Besides, I need you at home in July. I've been counting on not having to pay for day care while I'm working. Kids get the whole summer off but custodians don't!"

Melissa felt her chances sliding away. "There's a session in August I could go to. You're not working in August."

Sharlene looked at Jill. "I've already made plans for August. Jill's made us a wonderful offer."

Melissa didn't trust herself to speak.

"Jill's going to Europe for six weeks. Her brother's using their cabin at Flycatcher Lake in July, but no one's going to be there in August. So she's offered it to us. We get a holiday and we'll give up the apartment so we'll save a whole month's rent."

Melissa stared at her mother. "What are you talking about? You can't just give up this apartment!"

"Why not?"

"What if we don't get another one?"

"We will. There's lots of vacancies in this town, and I've been thinking about moving anyway. I think we can afford something a little nicer. We'll line up a new place before we go."

"I like it here." Melissa could hear the stubbornness in her voice. And it wasn't even true. She hated the apartment. Nothing ever worked right. The fridge froze the lettuce, the baseboard heaters rattled, and just last night the cord for the blinds in her bedroom had snapped.

Then the first part of Sharlene's announcement sank in. Spend a whole month in a cabin at a place called Flycatcher Lake! When she could have been at art camp!

"It's the end of June in three days," said Sharlene. "I'll give our notice and we'll move out the end of July."

Jill spoke for the first time. "You'll like it there, Melissa. My sons adore it. It's real wilderness. The lake's warm enough to swim in, and we have a canoe. There's even an island to explore. And the cabin is rustic but it's cozy."

"It'll be a holiday," said Sharlene. "It will be great for Cody. I used to love going to my grandpa's cabin in northern Ontario when I was a kid."

"I know. You've told me," muttered Melissa.

It was the only part of Sharlene's childhood that her mother would talk about. She had spent every summer at the cabin until she was twelve and her grandpa had a heart attack and had to sell the place. Melissa had always thought it sounded like a survival test. As far as she could tell, all Sharlene had done was yank hooks out of fish, swim in a lake full of leeches and battle black flies.

Sharlene took a final drag on her cigarette and stubbed it out in the saucer. "My last one."

Melissa pulled herself away from a horrifying picture of being stuck in a rustic cabin with her brother and mother. "*What*?"

"My last cigarette. As of right now, I've quit."

"Really." Melissa's voice was cold. "I thought

quitting smoking was supposed to be hard."

"It's very hard. At least I think it's going to be. But if I can quit booze and men, I can quit cigarettes."

Melissa's cheeks flamed. She hated it when her mother said things like that. But Jill didn't seem embarrassed. She raised her coffee mug. "Hear, hear!" she said. "To a new life!"

"To a new life!" said Sharlene.

Melissa turned around and flew out of the kitchen. She slammed the door of the bedroom she shared with Cody and threw herself on her bed. Her mother was always talking about their new life. Ever since the fire two years ago.

Melissa's tears poured out. It was unfair. When Sharlene talked about their new life, it made Melissa feel hopeful. Maybe things really would change. Some things *were* better, she had to admit. Sharlene's boyfriend Darren was gone and that was no loss. Sharlene wouldn't touch even a drop of alcohol anymore. But the money problems were still there. And when Sharlene worked, Melissa had more responsibilities at home and with Cody than ever.

She sat up and tore the brochure about art camp into tiny pieces. She would never ever want to go back to the way they were before the fire. But feeling hopeful and then being let down so hard was worse than not caring in the first place.

Two

Sharlene said she had packing down to a fine art. That's because we move so much, Melissa thought. Huntley was the third town Melissa had lived in, and Huntley Elementary was the fourth school she had been to. After the fire, Melissa had been sure they would leave Huntley, but instead Darren had left. Sharlene had announced that, as part of their new life, it was time they put down some roots.

Now the school principal offered to store their stuff in his garage. In July, Melissa babysat Cody during the long days while Sharlene was at school. In the evenings she helped fill the cardboard boxes that threatened to take over the apartment.

The boxes that Sharlene had written *Storage* on in black felt pen grew in a steady pile in the hallway. You had to turn sideways to edge your way past. Melissa made sure all the lids were securely taped down. She didn't want anyone poking around and seeing their junky stuff.

The boxes marked for the cabin at the lake stayed in the living room. They slowly filled with blue jeans, shorts, beach towels, socks and T-shirts. Pretty soon Melissa had trouble finding something to wear.

One afternoon Sharlene took Melissa and Cody to see the new apartment she had found. It was in a modern block at the other end of town. The present tenant, who was moving out in the middle of August, let them have a peek inside. Melissa got an impression of big airy rooms and lots of sunlight coming in the windows. It was better than anything she could have dreamed of. But she just shrugged when Sharlene asked her what she thought. She didn't really believe they were actually going to live there. Something was sure to go wrong.

The old apartment was stifling. Melissa slept under only a sheet, and even then she was drenched with sweat. Cody's whining became out of control. Sometimes Sharlene sat on the edge of Cody's bed and wiped his scarlet face with a cool damp facecloth.

"Just think. Pretty soon we'll be swimming in a real lake every day," she said. When she said things like that, Melissa caught herself listening. Then she reminded herself that nothing Sharlene had ever planned had turned out well.

It was weird to see her mother without a cigarette in her hand. In the evenings after supper, Sharlene drank cups of coffee steadily, and Melissa could sometimes hear her in the middle of the night roaming around the apartment. When she had gone exactly one month cigarette-free, Jill Templeton came over and they celebrated with cheesecake and a sparkling apple drink that looked like wine but wasn't. They all drank some out of wine glasses, even Cody.

One night Jill brought over all kinds of stuff for the cabin, including mosquito coils, bug spray, bottles of lamp oil, a secondhand campstove to replace the broken one, and spare flashlight batteries. Melissa got sick of her mother screeching over each item as if it were a long-lost friend. "Oh my god…my grandpa had a campstove just like that…I remember playing flashlight games on the ceiling with my sister…"

Jill told them more about Flycatcher Lake. "It's almost a mile long and kind of shaped like a banana. It's mostly wilderness. There are four cabins, including ours. I'm afraid August is going to be quiet this year. I think you'll be the only ones there."

Even Sharlene looked a little alarmed, and Jill added hastily, "You won't be entirely alone. The Hopes have a ranch at the end of the lake."

"Any kids?" said Sharlene. About six months earlier she had suddenly realized that Melissa never hung out with anybody, and she never gave up trying to find friends for her.

"An older boy and a girl about Melissa's age called Alice, but…" Jill hesitated.

"But she's weird," supplied Melissa.

Sharlene frowned at her.

"Not exactly weird," said Jill. "The whole family is a bit…well, reclusive. I've heard they've had some problems, but I'm not sure what exactly. They keep to themselves, but they'll be there if you have an emergency."

Melissa took a can of bug spray away from Cody, who was about to try it out on his hair. She read the label out loud. "*Effective against mosquitoes, black flies, ticks, fleas, gnats and chiggers.*"

Sharlene and Jill laughed as if it was the funniest thing they had ever heard, but Melissa didn't. What on earth were chiggers? They sounded disgusting.

Jill offered Sharlene the use of her truck. "It's four-wheel drive, and you'll need that to get in to the cabin. It's pretty rough."

Melissa held her breath. It was her mother's last chance to back out of this, to say it was all a horrible

13

mistake. She peered at Sharlene hopefully and then her shoulders sagged.

Sharlene's grin was enormous. It was one of the few times that Melissa had ever seen her mother look truly happy.

They left for Flycatcher Lake on the first of August in the baking hot afternoon. The back of the truck was filled with duffel bags and boxes of various sizes and shapes. As well, there were three cartons of groceries and two large coolers, borrowed from Jill, containing orange juice, margarine, eggs, milk, yogurt and cheese packed around blocks of ice.

After a couple of hours, they pulled off the highway at a rest stop to eat ham sandwiches and pieces of carrot cake, the icing melting on their fingers. Hot and sticky, they got back in the truck and continued on their way, Cody crammed in between Sharlene and Melissa.

Melissa leaned against the open window, freeing her hair from its ponytail and letting it blow outside as she watched the highway slide by. The hot vinyl seat stuck to her bare legs, and her back prickled with sweat. Sharlene, who had announced that she now had the hang of the truck, drove quickly, belting out the words to "King of the Road." "*No phone, no pool, no pets…I ain't got no ciii-ga-rettes…*"

Melissa wished she still had her iPod. It had been her Christmas present, the most expensive gift she had ever got. She knew her mother had made a lot of sacrifices to buy it, and she had been terrified a month later when she had to tell her that someone at school had stolen it from her backpack. Sharlene had been predictably furious—not at Melissa but at the unknown thief—and Melissa knew that there was no hope of Sharlene scraping up the money for another one.

Cody squirmed in his seat and said, for the hundredth time, "Are we almost there?" Every time he asked, Sharlene answered him patiently, telling him how many kilometers were left, which anyone could see was pointless because five minutes later he asked all over again.

This time Sharlene said, "We're almost at the turnoff. You watch for a sign that says Bear Creek."

"Like he can read," muttered Melissa. Cody's running shoe banged against her shin and she gave him a shove, then hunched further into her corner. She couldn't wait to get out of this furnace of a truck.

"*Third boxcar, midnight train…Desss-tination Bangor, Maine…,*" sang Sharlene.

"Mom, *please*," said Melissa.

Sharlene slammed on the brakes and turned right off the highway onto a gravel road. "My navigators are sleeping on the job!" she said. She drove over a cattle guard and along the road for half a kilometer and then stopped in front of a log building with a wide porch. A sign hung on chains from the eaves. *Bear Creek General Store Established 1916.*

"This is the end of civilization for us," she said. "Let's make the most of it!"

Melissa unglued her legs and climbed out of the truck. Cody slid out after her. "I have to go pee," he whined.

Sharlene glanced around vaguely. "There must be a washroom somewhere…come on, let's go inside and see what we can find."

A bell tinkled when they opened the door. Melissa had never seen such a cluttered store. Three long aisles were crammed with goods. Cereal, cookies, bags of sugar and boxes of pasta were mixed in with things like flashlights, bottles of detergent, fishing gear and mops. Two tall coolers stood against one wall, one with soft drinks and water and the other with milk and cheese in the top, and eggs, a basket of tomatoes and a few heads of lettuce in the bottom. A thin woman with short straight gray hair was reading a magazine at the counter at the back of the store.

Sharlene gave her a dazzling smile and said, "We need a washroom desperately for this little fellow."

Really, all Cody had said was that he had to go. Now he seemed to have forgotten all about it as he made a beeline for a row of jars filled with candy. The woman reached up to a hook on the wall and took down a key attached to a wooden horseshoe. "Washroom's around the back. Lock it when you're done."

Sharlene said, "Be an angel, Mel, and take him. I want to pick up a few things."

Melissa dragged Cody out of the store and back into the blistering heat. She found two doors, one that said *Colts* and another that said *Fillies*. She unlocked the *Colts* door and pushed Cody inside, ordering him to wait for her when he was done. Then she went into the *Fillies* and splashed cold water over her face and twisted her limp hair into a braid.

When they went back into the store, Sharlene was piling boxes of macaroni and cheese on the counter. "Look at all the caps hanging on the ceiling. Isn't it wild? This is Marge. She and her husband bought the store twenty years ago. Marge, this is Melissa and Cody."

Melissa flushed. Sharlene had probably told Marge their whole life story by now, every dismal detail. She pretended to be interested in a display of crocheted Kleenex boxes that looked like turtles. A sign in front of them said *Local Crafts*.

Melissa picked up a wooden carving of a duck and examined it. She suddenly felt conscious of Marge staring at her hand, and she put the bird down quickly, her cheeks hot. After the fire, her right hand had required three skin grafts. Sharlene said she was too sensitive, but Melissa could tell when people first noticed the tight puckered skin. They stared right at it and then they pretended that they hadn't seen it, and she could tell they were embarrassed.

"Get yourself something to drink, sweetie," said Sharlene. "You look like you're roasting." She consulted a crumpled piece of paper. "Let's see...one last thing, a fishing permit."

"There's shrimp bait in the freezer," said Marge.

Two men came in, wearing blue jeans with no shirts. One was short with a beard and the other was tall with a tattoo of a dragon on his arm. They eyed Sharlene right away and Melissa felt her stomach tighten. "We'll take two cases of Labatt's beer, Marge," said the man with the tattoo, who reminded Melissa a little bit of Darren. He winked at Sharlene.

Melissa took an icy can of Coke out of the cooler and asked Marge, "Is it okay if I drink it now before we pay for it?"

"Sure," said Marge, and Melissa took it outside and slumped down on a wooden bench. She took a long sip and concentrated on the fizziness, letting her mind drain.

The men left with their beer, and after a while Cody came out clutching a small brown candy bag, his cheek sticking out in a lump. Marge and Sharlene followed him, chatting like old friends. Marge leaned against the railing and lit a cigarette.

"Follow this road for about nine kilometers," she said. A truck drove by, dust swirling under its tires. A woman in the passenger's seat waved and Marge waved back. "You'll come to the Flying Horse Guest Ranch. You can't miss the sign. Bonnie and Gord Hill run it. They'll be your neighbors. They're nice people, and they'll help you out if you have a problem."

"Jill Templeton said there was a ranch at the end of the lake as well," said Sharlene. "Owned by the Hope family."

There was a short silence. "The Hopes don't really like people coming around," said Marge. "You'd be better off relying on Bonnie and Gord."

Melissa drained the last of her Coke and studied Marge over the rim of the can. Jill had said the Hopes were reclusive, but Marge made it sound like there was something else. What exactly was wrong with them? Well, she had no intention of hanging around with the girl anyway—Alice or whatever her name was.

"As soon as you pass the Flying Horse sign, start looking for a grassy road to the left. That's your only way in to the Templetons' cabin. There's a better road around the other side of the lake but it only goes to the Hopes' ranch. It's a good thing you've got four-wheel drive. You'll need it."

"Great," said Sharlene. She slid a couple of bags into the back of the truck and slammed the tailgate shut.

"Remember, no campfires until the ban is lifted," said Marge. "The fire hazard is at the top of the scale." She stubbed out her cigarette in a chipped saucer. "Too hot even to smoke. The road's right after the guest ranch. You can't miss it."

"Got it," said Sharlene. "Hop in, Cody. I don't want to be looking for this cabin in the dark."

As usual, Sharlene was exaggerating. Melissa didn't think it was going to be dark for ages. The sun was still blazing down on them from a cloudless blue sky. She climbed in after Cody and leaned against the seat with a feeling of looming disaster. You can't miss it, Marge had said. She didn't know Sharlene's luck.

Melissa watched her mother tuck the fishing license in the visor. She frowned. "Why did you pretend you're interested in fishing when you're not?"

"How do you know what I'm interested in?" Sharlene waved out the window as she headed down the gravel road. "I like Marge," she said.

"You just met her," Melissa pointed out.

"I know that, Miss Precise," said Sharlene. "But I still like her. We'll be using the store a lot, and I think we're going to become good friends."

"You say that about everybody," said Melissa. "I suppose you also liked the man with the tattoo."

"Melissa!" Sharlene exploded suddenly, and Melissa cringed. "You're pushing it, young lady."

"Okay. I'm sorry," muttered Melissa. She stared out the window at the forest that crowded both sides of the road. She would ignore her mother and concentrate instead on making sure they didn't get lost.

Three

Sharlene drove past the grassy road three times before they figured out that it even *was* a road. "This has got to be it," she said, turning onto a narrow track that disappeared into the forest. She fiddled for a moment with a lever near the floor and the truck jerked into four-wheel drive.

For the next ten minutes they bounced over ruts and through potholes. Branches swiped the sides of the truck, and Melissa closed the window so she wouldn't get hit. Then the trees parted and a meadow shimmered like a golden sea on the right side of the road. A deer with pricked ears stood in the long grass, watching them pass. "Lovely," breathed Sharlene, while Cody nearly climbed on top of Melissa screaming, "Let me see!"

They drove back into the shady forest. "We should pass three other cabins before we get to ours," said Sharlene. "We're at the very end of the road."

The truck lurched over a deep pothole, and Melissa grabbed the door handle to steady herself. She glimpsed water glinting between the trees. "There's the first one," she said, staring at a small cabin made of weathered gray boards. It was their first proper view of the lake and Sharlene slowed the truck so they could have a good look. In front of the cabin the water was a dark emerald green, but farther out it was speckled with bright sunlight.

They passed two more cabins. One was tall and thin with an upper story, and the other had a shiny tin roof. The road veered away from the lake for a few minutes and then turned back toward the water, coming to a sudden end at a grassy clearing beside a log cabin.

"This must be it," said Sharlene. She pulled up beside a tree and turned off the truck. "Okay, everybody out!"

They climbed stiffly out of the truck. Sharlene gave a huge stretch. Melissa's heart thudded as she looked around. They were going to spend a whole month here?

The cabin was long and narrow. Tall pine trees sheltered the back and sides. At the front was a porch and below that an expanse of dry brown grass that sloped right to the edge of the lake. A dock jutted out into the water, with an overturned red canoe resting on the end. Straight across from them on the other side of the lake, the sun blazed low in the sky, ready to dip behind a steep forested hillside. Melissa used her hands to shade her eyes from the glare on the water. A little way down the lake, she could see a small island covered in trees.

A squirrel chattered shrilly in the branches above her, making her jump. She hugged her arms to her chest while Sharlene opened the screen door on the side of the cabin and fiddled with a key. Silently she followed Sharlene and Cody inside.

Melissa had a first impression of dark log walls, a big black woodstove that she had to step around and a thick musty smell. Then Sharlene pulled back the curtains on the two big front windows and opened a door in between that led out to the porch. The setting sun streamed in.

The room was filled with furniture: a kitchen table with chairs, an old saggy couch with a plaid blanket draped over the back, a rocking chair and a couple of armchairs. There was a brown counter with wooden cupboards above and below. Assorted raincoats and thick fleeces hung on hooks beside the door. In one corner there was a rubber mat with a pair of boots on it, and under the windows were shelves with rows of paperback books, board games and jigsaw puzzles. At the end were two small bedrooms, their doors open. Melissa spotted bunk beds in one and a double bed in the other.

"It smells in here," said Cody. His face puckered in a frown.

"I don't think so," said Sharlene.

"Yes, it does," said Cody. "It stinks."

Sharlene gave an exaggerated sniff. "Oh, that. That's cabin smell. All cabins smell like this. My grandpa's cabin in Ontario smelled just the same."

Cody stuck his thumb in his mouth. Sharlene surveyed the room calmly. "The windows have screens, thank goodness. Let's get some air in here. It's like an oven."

Melissa watched while Sharlene opened windows. She felt stuck to the floor, unable to move. The cabin was even smaller than their apartment. They would be living on top of each other.

Sharlene had disappeared into one of the bedrooms. "I haven't slept in a bunk bed since Grandpa's," she called out. "If you don't mind, Mel, Cody and I will take this room."

For a second, Melissa thought she hadn't heard right. Cody was going to share with their mother? Ever since he was two, he had slept in Melissa's room.

"You can think about fixing up your room tomorrow," said Sharlene.

"Fix it up with what?" said Melissa. She tried to wrap her mind around the amazing news that she had her very own room.

"Maybe some of your drawings. You're the artist—Oh!" Sharlene said suddenly.

"What is it?" said Melissa. She stood in the doorway.

"There's a broken window in here. Look! It looks like someone smashed it with a rock. There's glass all over the floor." Sharlene peered outside. "The screen's lying out there on the ground. What on earth would have caused that?"

"The mosquitoes are coming in," said Melissa. She tried to grab a mosquito that drifted near her cheek.

Sharlene pushed back a strand of hair. She looked tired. "I'll pop that screen back on. Then let's get our stuff out of the truck. We'll just bring it in. We don't have to unpack everything tonight. And we can sweep up this glass later."

Sharlene retrieved the screen and snapped it back into place, and then they made trips back and forth from the truck to the cabin until everything was stacked inside. Sharlene made a halfhearted attempt at organizing. "Kitchen stuff and food against that wall, duffel bags in the bedrooms…"

Melissa set a box labeled *Cody* in the room with the bunk beds and then carried a box that said *Melissa* into her bedroom. Sharlene had gone on and on about taking enough things to the lake so they didn't get bored and had instructed them each to fill a box with stuff to do. Cody's box was full of his Duplo building set, action figures, a marble game and other toys. Melissa had packed mostly art supplies, library books and a needlepoint kit of a wolf that she had bought at a flea market.

Melissa pushed her box against the wall. She shut the door and stood for a minute in the middle of the room. Her own space. Cody was definitely not allowed in.

She checked it out thoroughly. The bed, which looked soft and lumpy, was covered by a faded yellow and orange quilt. The only other furniture was a blue dresser with four empty drawers that stuck when you pulled them. A cupboard with folding doors contained a bunch of coat hangers, a life jacket, an extra blanket and a pair of worn slippers. A pale orange curtain covered the one small window. Two of the walls were log and the other two were made out of brown boards. A calendar, open to July, with a photograph of a bald eagle, hung beside the bed.

Melissa took the calendar down and stuck it on the shelf in the cupboard. She wanted to start from the beginning with her room, like a piece of fresh drawing paper. She pulled back the curtain and gazed out at the lake and the dock with the red canoe. She opened the window wide to let in some air, and a sweet pine smell drifted inside. She was just thinking about putting some of her stuff in the drawers when Sharlene called from the other room, "Mel, I need you to get some water for supper."

What was that about? Then Melissa remembered that Jill had explained that there was no running water in the cabin. Water for dishes and washing up came from an outside well with a hand pump. Melissa hadn't really thought about it at the time but she did now. No water in the cabin also meant an outhouse. Yuck.

Sharlene gave Melissa a plastic water container and she went out the side door, the screen door banging behind her. The sun had disappeared behind the hill, and the lake was as dark and smooth as a pane of glass. She found the pump behind the cabin, near a lean-to shed filled with firewood. She studied it for a minute, trying to figure out how it worked. She gave the handle an experimental tug. It was stiff and she pulled harder, yanking it up and down half a dozen times before the water finally splashed out of the pipe, soaking her runners.

The problem was, the water gushed out in spurts, going everywhere except into the narrow opening of the container. When the container was finally half full, Melissa quit pumping, her arms aching, and carried it back to the cabin.

Cody was stretched out on the couch, sucking his thumb. "It's far too hot to light the woodstove," said Sharlene. She set up the campstove on the counter.

Melissa watched silently while her mother attached the propane tank and lit the burner with a match. "How did you know how to do that?" she asked.

"Jill gave me a lesson." Sharlene poured water into a big pot and set it on the burner. "How does macaroni and cheese sound? You can set out the dishes. And maybe open up a can of peaches for dessert."

Melissa rummaged through the cupboards. There were all sorts of mismatched plates, bowls and mugs. She put out three plates and three mugs, two made of blue pottery with loons on the sides and a red plastic mug for Cody. Then she hunted for a can opener.

"There's no can opener," she announced after digging through the drawers.

"How could a cabin like this not have a can opener?" mused Sharlene. "Luckily we brought one of our own." With one eye on the campstove, she produced a can opener from the top of a cardboard box.

Macaroni and cheese was Cody's favorite meal, but when it was ready he flipped macaroni out of his bowl and yelled that the only thing he could eat was a hot dog. Then he burst into tears when Sharlene said she had forgotten to bring ketchup.

Cody said he hated peaches because they were too slimy. Sharlene made him a piece of bread and jam, which he promptly threw on the floor. "Someone is exhausted," she said. She put down her fork, got up from the table and scooped Cody up in her arms. He stiffened and kicked her legs with his feet, then went as limp as a rag doll. "Come on, buddy boy, we'll find this outhouse and then it's time to crash."

Melissa frowned. She couldn't understand why Sharlene let Cody act like such a baby. In the old days, Sharlene was mad at Cody all the time. Melissa could remember Sharlene screaming at him and Cody throwing himself on the floor, shrieking at the top of his lungs. It was like Sharlene was trying to be the perfect mother now.

With a sigh, Melissa got up and scraped Cody's macaroni off the table and into a plastic bag. Then she picked up the piece of bread and jam and threw it on top. Jill had warned them about not letting the bears get into the garbage, but she couldn't remember what they were supposed to do with it, so she left it on the counter.

The cabin was filling with shadows and pretty soon they wouldn't be able to see a thing. Melissa heard Sharlene's and Cody's voices outside the window, and in a moment they were back inside. Sharlene said the mosquitoes were out in droves, and Cody announced sleepily that he had almost fallen into the outhouse hole. He insisted on being carried into the bedroom.

A moment later Melissa heard Cody scream "No! Go away! GO AWAY!" and then Sharlene was back. "He wants you," she said.

Melissa avoided the wounded look in her mother's eyes. For the first few years of his life, Melissa had been the one to put Cody to bed at night while Sharlene and Darren drank beer in front of the TV or partied with their friends in the trailer next door. Right after the fire, he had clung to Melissa tighter than ever until sometimes the only way she could get him to sleep was to rock him like a baby. Lately he had been better, allowing Sharlene to tuck him in most nights, but when he was overtired he demanded Melissa.

Melissa had heard Sharlene and Jill talking about it one night. "They push me away," Sharlene had said, her voice tight, "both of them. My god, it's been two years. Sometimes this whole motherhood thing feels as fragile as a piece of glass."

"It *is* fragile," Jill had replied in the no-nonsense tone that Melissa remembered from grade four.

"Melissa and Cody have some legitimate reasons not to trust you. Don't expect miracles overnight."

Melissa went into the bedroom. Cody was lying on the bottom bunk in his underpants, with a sheet crumpled around his feet. Sharlene had put a small red flashlight on the dresser beside him. Melissa turned it on and gave it to him. "Everyone gets their own flashlight. This is yours." She let him shine it on the walls for a few minutes and then switched it off. He rolled over on his side, his chest rising and falling with his soft breath.

Melissa stayed until she was sure he was asleep before she left, shutting the bedroom door quietly behind her. "You shouldn't carry him places," she said to Sharlene. She could hear the criticism in her voice, as sharp as a knife, but she couldn't stop herself. "He's four years old. He's big enough to walk."

"He does walk," said Sharlene. "Just not tonight."

"And I don't think you should have got him the bread. He's always loved macaroni and cheese."

"Well, I guess he doesn't anymore." Sharlene sounded worn out.

Melissa gave up. "So now what?" she said.

"What do you mean, now what?"

"What are we going to do now? It's going to be pitch-dark in here soon."

"Well," said Sharlene, "we could figure out how to light the oil lamps. Then we could heat up some water on the campstove and wash these dishes. Or we could just go to bed and do it all tomorrow."

"Bed," said Melissa quickly. She couldn't wait to sleep in her room without Cody. "Where is this outhouse anyway?"

"There's a little path between the trees behind the woodshed. Wait till you see the stars. They're amazing."

Melissa got her flashlight and went outside. She stood by the door, stunned. The sky was like a giant black bowl filled to the brim with dazzling stars. There must be *millions*, she thought. Her mother was right. They *were* amazing. They were much more brilliant than the stars she saw in town. She tilted her head back until she was dizzy.

Her trip to the outhouse turned out to be definitely gross and full of mosquitoes but not as bad as she had imagined.

Before she went back to the cabin, Melissa walked down to the lake. She beamed the flashlight ahead of her onto the dock. Something stuck in between the boards glinted in the light. Melissa bent down and picked up a silver chain. It was a bracelet with a silver letter, a capital *A*, in the middle. Melissa studied it for a moment and then slipped it in her pocket.

Suddenly a long eerie cry quavered across the water, making the back of her neck tingle.

Wait until you hear the loons, Jill had said. There's a pair that nests on the lake. They make the most incredible wailing sound. It'll give you goose bumps.

Melissa was pretty sure she had just heard her first loon. She held her breath, hoping to hear it again, but there was only a deep still silence. It made Melissa feel tiny, as if she were the only person on the whole planet. She waited a few more minutes and then swatted at a mosquito and headed up the dry grassy slope to the dark cabin.

Four

Flames crawled across the carpet and swept up the curtains in a torrent of orange and red. Melissa tried to scream but she couldn't make a sound. She heard Darren shout, "What the *hell* is happening?" and then there was a roaring noise. She couldn't tell if Darren was inside or outside the trailer, and she had no idea where Sharlene and Cody were. There was too much smoke. It was billowing around her, making her choke. She needed to get up and look for Cody but there was something wrong with her legs.

Her eyes snapped open. Her heart was hammering in her chest, and her back was soaked with sweat. It took her a few seconds to realize that she had been dreaming. Relief flooded through her like water.

The counselor, a woman at the Family Help Center in Huntley, had told Melissa to take deep slow breaths when she had the fire dream. *One, two, three, breathe.* She had also said that the dreams would stop if Melissa talked about things instead of keeping everything bottled up inside her. She ended up making Melissa cry every time they went to see her, until Sharlene said with tight lips that they weren't going to come anymore. Besides, wasn't it better to talk to your own mother instead of a stranger?

The problem was, Melissa couldn't talk to Sharlene about the fire. She had tried but it just didn't work.

Now her breathing was back to normal and her heart had slowed down. She reached for her flashlight on the floor and switched it on. She shone it on the log walls. She remembered a building set someone had given her when she was a little kid. You could stack the tiny logs together and make cabins just like this one. Cody would have loved it, but like everything else it had been destroyed in the fire.

It was weird not to hear Cody breathing beside her or music blaring from another apartment or a car door slamming outside. The apartment was never absolutely quiet, like it was here.

The air wafting through the window was cool. Melissa pulled the quilt, which she had shoved to the bottom of the bed, up around her shoulders and drifted back to sleep.

The next time Melissa woke up, her room was full of light, and breakfast noises were coming through the door: a cupboard door shutting, Cody's high-pitched voice demanding something, the lid on a pot rattling. She smelled coffee and bacon.

She made a trip to the outhouse and then sat at the table and devoured pancakes and maple syrup with strips of crispy bacon. Sharlene had left the windows open all night and the cabin was chilly. "Jill said it would cool off a lot at night," she said. "It's glorious after our apartment. But it looks like it's going to be a scorcher again today. There's not a cloud in the sky."

She heated water in a pot on the campstove and poured it into a plastic basin. Melissa washed the dishes, glancing out the window at the same time at the glassy lake. Sharlene got out toothbrushes and toothpaste and they brushed their teeth and spat into the basin, and then Melissa took it outside and dumped the dirty water into a pit behind the cabin.

The morning stretched ahead. Cody had spread his Duplo building blocks all over the floor, and Sharlene was scrubbing the insides of cupboards with a rag and putting away their cans of food.

"It's strange," Sharlene said. "Jill told me that it was a firm cabin rule to always leave some food behind for the next person to use when they come up—canned stuff that mice can't get into. But I don't see anything here. I feel like Mother Hubbard with her bare cupboards."

Melissa shrugged. She didn't see why they would want to eat someone else's food anyway.

"I'm wondering," said Sharlene slowly, "if someone has been in this cabin. The broken window, the missing food, no can opener. And I think there might be a sleeping bag missing too."

Melissa's heart gave a jump. There was no one around for miles if they needed help. "Do you think it could have been some kind of criminal?" she said nervously.

Sharlene glanced at her face and said quickly, "It's nothing to worry about, honey. If someone was here, they'll be long gone by now. Why don't you go outside and explore?"

Melissa wandered outside, but in a few minutes she had seen everything. What was she going to do all month? She went back inside the cabin to her room. She emptied out her duffel bag, filling the dresser drawers with her clothes, and then she opened up the box that said *Melissa*. She took out a sketchbook and a box of sketching pencils, then sat on the bed, propping herself against the pillow, and started to work on a picture of the cabin.

There was something relaxing about drawing logs. Melissa lost all track of time, which was what always happened when she was drawing. She worked all morning, paying special attention to the shading, and was pleased with the way the logs looked round. She drew the tall pine trees and put a squirrel on one of the branches. When she was finished, she hung the drawing on the nail where the calendar had been, poking a tiny hole in the paper.

She took out a new piece of paper and was trying to create in her mind a picture of the deer in the meadow when Sharlene called, "Hey, Mel, come and see this!"

Cody and Sharlene were crouched on the floor in front of an open cupboard. Melissa looked over their shoulders. They were staring at a glass jar. Something was moving in the bottom.

"It's a mouse," said Sharlene. "I don't know how long it's been in there. It must have been crawling along inside the cupboard and fallen in. The jar was at the back of this cupboard."

Melissa peered more closely at the jar. A tiny gray mouse was scrabbling around the sides.

"Let it out!" shrieked Cody.

"Not in here," said Sharlene. "We'll take it outside."

They trooped outdoors to a spot under a pine tree. Sharlene tipped the jar on its side and the mouse slid onto the ground. It lay there, a scruffy ball of matted fur.

"It's dead," said Cody.

"No, it's still alive. Its whiskers are quivering," said Sharlene.

The sun must be blinding, thought Melissa, after being in that dark cupboard for...how long? Days?

Suddenly the mouse stirred. It ran in tight little circles, like one of Cody's windup toys.

"What's it doing?" shouted Cody.

"It still thinks it's in the jar," said Sharlene. "How horrible. It must have been running around in there for ages."

Cody wanted to touch the mouse with a stick, but Sharlene pulled him back. Melissa held her breath, horrified, as the tiny mouse raced madly around. Gradually it spiraled out into bigger and bigger circles. Then it veered sideways into a clump of long grass and disappeared.

"Well," said Sharlene. She sounded shaken. "That was something."

Cody was rooting around in the grass, but the mouse had vanished. Melissa stored the picture of the mouse in her brain. She would try to draw it later and see if she could capture the desperation she had glimpsed in its tiny bright eyes.

Sharlene stood up. The sun was high over their heads, blazing down on them from a dark blue sky. "How about some lunch, guys?"

After a lunch of peanut-butter-and-jam sandwiches and lemonade, Melissa helped Sharlene unstack the lawn chairs at the end of the porch and drag them into a shady spot under some trees. Sharlene brought out a bin of toy cars with pieces of road and miniature bridges and tunnels for Cody and a book for herself. She stuck a cap on Cody's head and settled herself on a wooden recliner.

Melissa didn't feel like reading or drawing. She walked down to the end of the dock. She had never seen so much forest. You wouldn't even know there were any other cabins on the lake when you stood here. Jill was right when she called it wilderness.

She sat on the edge of the dock beside the canoe and dangled her bare feet in the lake. The water felt cold and silky. A school of tiny fish swam by, almost close enough to tickle her toes. She swished them away with her foot and then gazed across at the island. All around the edge, the dark forest was reflected in the smooth water, making a perfect mirror image. I could draw that, thought Melissa lazily. She had a vision of covering the bare walls of her little room with her pictures, like a mini gallery. It would be something to do for the rest of this long boring summer.

"Why don't you take the canoe out?" Sharlene called.

Melissa turned around. "What?"

"The canoe. I saw a paddle and life jackets up by the woodshed. Take it for a spin."

"I don't know how," said Melissa.

For a second, Melissa saw that look in her mother's eyes that meant she was frustrated with her. She hunched her shoulders. Sharlene always said Melissa didn't try, but it wasn't true. Melissa liked to take the time to think about something new instead of just plunging in.

"Come on," said Sharlene. She put her book down and stood up. "It's not rocket science. I paddled a canoe everywhere when I was at Grandpa's cabin."

"I want to," said Cody.

"Not this time," said Sharlene firmly. "Melissa gets the first turn."

It was settled then, thought Melissa resentfully. Whether she wanted to or not. She wished her mother would back off sometimes. But, she had to admit, a little part of her was excited to try the canoe.

Melissa protested that she would be too hot if she had to wear the life jacket. After a brief argument, Sharlene gave in as long as Melissa promised to keep it right beside her feet. *All those swimming lessons she forced me to take have paid off,* thought Melissa. Cody watched, his thumb in his mouth, while they each took an end of the canoe and flipped it over. They slid it off the dock into the water. Melissa grabbed the rope tied to the bow.

"This is great!" said Sharlene. "I feel like a kid again! Now, put a hand on either side and kind of hoist yourself in!"

The canoe wobbled back and forth wildly, and Melissa's heart gave a little jump. But she was in. She perched on the edge of a wooden seat. In front of her, the bow tipped up out of the water. Sharlene passed her the paddle.

"Take deep steady strokes," she said.

Melissa dragged the paddle through the water and the canoe shot forward. She dragged it again and started to veer in a circle.

"You're going to have to keep switching sides to go straight or…heck, I forgot all about the J stroke. You can paddle on one side if you use the J stroke," said Sharlene. "Come on back and I'll show you."

Melissa spun in a couple of circles until she got back to the dock. She handed the paddle to Sharlene and then held on to the edge of the dock so she wouldn't float away.

Sharlene gave a quick demonstration. She pulled the paddle back in the air and angled it away from her at the end of the stroke. "Pretend that you're making a letter J," she said. She gave the paddle back to Melissa.

Melissa had no idea her mother knew stuff like this. The J stroke was way harder than it looked, and the canoe zigzagged back and forth, but at least it didn't go in circles. She loved the way the canoe scooted across the water, and she loved the drippy line the paddle made when she carried it back to the start of each stroke.

Sharlene was grinning at her from the dock. Melissa turned and studied the island. It wasn't very far away. She bet she could be there in five minutes. "I'm going to the island," she shouted, feeling suddenly ready for anything.

Sharlene gave her a thumbs-up.

Five

The island was farther away than it looked. Melissa's arms started to ache, and the canoe had a mind of its own. She abandoned the J stroke and paddled on both sides, switching back and forth every ten strokes as she drew closer.

The forest grew right to the shore. There was no beach, just a jumble of boulders and overhanging bushes and logs. She headed toward a grassy bank that was partly cut away. A dead tree lay half on the ground and half submerged, its silver gray limbs sticking up like the ribs of a sea creature.

One more stroke and she was in the island's shadow, sliding from brilliant sunlight into a cool green world. She rested the paddle and glided the last few meters through a patch of green lily pads as flat as plates that rustled against the bottom of the canoe.

The water was clear and shallow. She could see the smooth humped backs of rocks and the long ropey stalks of the water lilies shooting up from the muddy bottom. She grabbed a low sweepy branch hanging over the water and pulled herself closer to shore. There was a scraping sound and the canoe bumped to a stop. She would have to wade the rest of the way.

She slipped her legs over the side and dropped into the ankle-deep water. Hanging on to the canoe, she picked her way carefully over the slippery rocks to the bow. She grabbed the rope and tied it to the branch. Then she scrambled up onto the bank.

Melissa grinned, exhilarated at being on an island for the first time in her life. She glanced across at the cabin. Sharlene, looking tiny, was standing on the end of the dock, waving both arms above her head. Melissa waved back.

She gazed around. It would be hard to go very far into the middle of the island. The trees grew close together and a tangle of underbrush, fallen logs and branches covered the ground. Then she realized that she was standing on a rough trail that looked like it followed the shore. She set off to explore, the ground prickly under her bare feet. The trail hugged the lake, gradually curving to the left out of the shade and into the bright sun. It was crisscrossed with tree roots and carpeted with brown pine needles.

Soon Melissa couldn't see their cabin anymore. Farther down the lake, a tin roof glinted in the sun. This end of the island was swampy, with tall bulrushes and more lily pads. The trail skirted the swamp and swept around to the left again, in and out of dappled sunlight.

In ten minutes she was on the other side of the island. Sometimes the trail disappeared and Melissa had to climb over boulders or around trees that had toppled half into the water, their massive branches blocking the way. She rounded a bend and stopped, her feet rooted to the ground in surprise.

A huge gray rock, as flat as a dining room table, jutted out over the water. In the middle was a striped beach towel with a backpack beside it. A paperback book lay facedown on the rock and a few other books were scattered about.

Melissa had been pretending that the island belonged to her, and she felt cold with shock. It was very quiet; the only sound was a bird chittering somewhere in a clump of willows. She didn't think there was anyone here but she couldn't be sure.

She swallowed. "Hello?" she called.

There was no answer. The bird fell silent, as though startled to have its peace disturbed.

"Hello?" she said again.

She waited for a few breathless moments. Then she climbed onto the rock and crouched down to examine the books. She scanned the titles. *The Last King, The Warrior's Triumph, Siege at Midnight, Quest for Fire.* The books were thick, like something an adult would read. The covers showed weird monsters and people in armor holding shields and brandishing swords.

Melissa stood up. She had spotted something leaning against a tree at the edge of the forest. She jumped off the rock and walked over to look at it. It was a handmade bow, fashioned from a long stick that had been bent into an arc. The bark had been peeled off and the creamy yellow wood gleamed like satin. There was a piece of string tied tightly from one end to the other.

Was it a real bow? Melissa couldn't see any arrows. She glanced around, suddenly feeling nervous. Something caught her eye. She stared at a clump of reeds at the edge of the lake, taking a few seconds to realize what she was looking at—the side of a blue canoe.

Prickles shot up her spine. The person who owned all this stuff must be somewhere on the island right now, maybe even hiding close by in the trees, watching her. Melissa spun around and ran back along the trail, scrambling over the boulders and logs. She tripped over a root and sprawled on the ground, feeling a sharp sting in her knee. Shakily she got up and kept running, not stopping until she was back at her canoe.

She stood there for a moment, catching her breath. Then she untied the rope and climbed in, her heart thumping wildly. She hated the thought of someone spying on her. More than anything, she wanted to get away.

Six

Melissa hugged her secret for the rest of the day. When Sharlene asked her about the island, she shrugged and said there was nothing much there, just a lot of rocks and fallen trees and thick forest. She might go back, she said casually. There were a few things she wanted to sketch.

She wasn't exactly sure why she didn't want to tell her mother what she had seen. It had something to do with Sharlene's eagerness to find her a friend. Sharlene would probably want to go over to the island herself and find out who it was and introduce Melissa and tell the stranger her whole life story.

Melissa had figured out that the owner of the books and the bow must be the boy from the ranch at the end of the lake. She was pretty sure Jill had said that the girl, Alice, had a brother, and the books and the bow definitely looked like boy stuff. Besides, there was no one else on the lake it could be. Jill had said the people in the other cabins weren't coming up this August.

That big flat rock would be a great place to go to get away from Cody's pestering. She could take her drawing book. She wondered if the boy went there every day. She hoped not. She formed a tentative plan to find out. She could paddle right around the island and then she could see the rock from the safety of the canoe.

Cody went to bed right after supper, exhausted, cranky and sunburned after his day outside. Sharlene dug through the boxes of games on the shelf and pulled out Monopoly.

"What are you doing?" said Melissa. She couldn't remember ever playing a board game with Sharlene. Besides, she had really gashed her knee when she had fallen and it was aching, and the tops of her shoulders were burned so badly they were scarlet. "I don't like board games, and Monopoly's no fun with two people anyway."

Sharlene was undaunted. She put Monopoly back and pulled out another box and studied it for a minute. "This is called Boggle. It's not a board game and it's meant for two people."

Melissa hated it when her mother got that over-eager look on her face. She had planned to start another drawing for her bedroom wall, maybe of the mouse. She flopped down at the table. "One game," she said. "That's all."

Inside the box there were pencils, a tray with a clear plastic cover full of dice with letters on them instead of numbers, a tiny hourglass and a pad of blank paper. Melissa sketched a miniature log cabin in the corner of the top sheet while Sharlene scanned the rules.

"Okay, got it," Sharlene said finally. She explained the rules quickly. It sounded boring. You had to shake the tray to mix up the dice and then look at the letters on top and write down all the words you could find before the sand in the hourglass ran out.

Melissa tore off two sheets of paper, one for her and one for Sharlene. Her mother put the lid over the tray and gave it a vigorous shake, scattering the little cubes. She wiggled the tray so the cubes would settle back into their holes and then removed the lid. She turned over the hourglass. "Okay, go."

All Melissa could see were stupid little words like *it* and *saw* and *for*. She wrote them down, trying not to pay attention to Sharlene, who was scribbling madly. She glanced at the sand; there was just a trickle left. She looked back at the cubes and the word *settle* jumped out at her. She felt a spark of triumph as she wrote it down. Six letters—that might even be a record.

They tallied up the score quickly, arguing over Sharlene's word *bummer*. "It might have been a word when you were a kid," said Melissa, "but nobody says that today."

"Dictionary, we need a dictionary," said Sharlene, but a quick hunt through the shelves didn't produce one.

"We're not accepting it," said Melissa firmly. It turned out that *settle* gave her bonus points and she declared herself the winner.

"Rematch," said Sharlene.

They played two more games, winning one each. The light inside the cabin grew dim, and Sharlene called a brief halt to light a couple of oil lamps. The soft flames flickered on the log walls, shutting out the night. Three more games and then Melissa, her eyes drooping with sleep, said she wanted to go to bed.

She packed everything back in the box and put it away on the shelf. Sharlene was humming and she looked happy. Melissa analyzed her own feelings. Boggle was okay. Well…even a little bit fun, she had to admit. She just hoped her mother didn't think she was going to play games with her every night.

At breakfast, Sharlene announced her plan. "You entertain Cody in the mornings while I'm working on my course. Then in the afternoons it'll be my shift and you're free to do what you want."

Melissa looked up from her bowl of Cheerios. The ice had already melted in the coolers and the milk was lukewarm. "You're not really doing that course, are you?"

"I certainly am. English Eleven. I've got all the materials. They arrived just before we left."

The English course had been Jill's idea. Sharlene had dropped out of high school halfway through grade eleven. Jill had urged Sharlene to upgrade slowly, a course at a time through distance education, and get her graduation diploma. English Eleven was a good place to start.

Sharlene had been uncertain. Melissa, skeptical that her mother could even do it, had forgotten all about it. Silently, she poured more Cheerios into Cody's bowl.

"It's going to be a lot of reading. Short stories and novels," said Sharlene. "And writing essays I think."

"Mmmm," said Melissa. Did Sharlene think this was going to impress her? She frowned. She didn't really like the idea of having to look after Cody all morning. In Huntley there was the playground in the park to take him to and the little kids' story hour at the library. And of course there was always the TV.

"I even have to read a play by Shakespeare. My god, can you believe that? Me?" Sharlene sounded more excited than worried.

Melissa sighed. "I know what I'll do with Cody," she said.

"What?" demanded Cody through a mouthful of cereal. Milk dribbled down his chin.

Melissa eyed him critically. "I'm going to teach you how to swim."

Sharlene said she was going to run to the store for more ice. At first she wanted them all to go, but the thought of bouncing over that rough road again didn't thrill Melissa. Besides, she knew her mother. She would be there for ages, talking to her new best friend Marge. Finally Sharlene agreed that Melissa and Cody could stay at the cabin as long as they absolutely promised not to go in the water until she got back.

Melissa dragged Cody's box out of the bedroom and parked him in the middle of the floor. Sharlene had put a few new things in there: a bag of plastic jungle animals and a dump truck that he could load with his building blocks. Melissa prayed that, for a little while anyway, it would keep his attention. She settled herself at the table with her drawing book and her box of sketching pencils.

For once Cody was an angel, even thanking her and not spilling anything when she made him a snack of juice and cookies. She was absorbed in her mouse drawing and was surprised when she heard Sharlene honk the horn to say she was back.

Sharlene admired Melissa's drawing and said she had captured the mouse's fear exactly. She chatted while she put away some groceries. "There's a fair here every August," she said. "I picked up an entry form. It's the old-fashioned kind, you know, where people enter their jars of jam and quilts and they're judged. Marge said there's a section for kids. You could put in some of your drawings."

Melissa shrugged. Her drawings were private and she couldn't imagine displaying them at a fair. She didn't even like it when the teacher put all their artwork up on the wall at school.

"Well, we'll see," said Sharlene, which was what she always said when she thought Melissa was being stubborn. "Now I'm going to get to work. Good luck with the swimming lesson."

She needed more than good luck, Melissa discovered quickly. She needed a miracle. Cody refused to go in over his knees and screamed when Melissa splashed a tiny bit of water on his chest. He was mesmerized by the tiny fish and spent the rest of the lesson trying to catch them with a stick.

When lunch was finished, Melissa didn't feel at all guilty about handing Cody over to Sharlene for the afternoon. After all, it had been her idea.

Melissa's arms were still sore from the previous day's paddling, but the canoe behaved much better now. She headed right to the swamp at the far end of the island. She paddled through reeds that were taller than her head. It was like moving through a bowl of soup, she thought, as the canoe went slower and slower. She rested for a few minutes, enjoying the feeling of being completely hidden in a green jungle. Then she gave a few hard long strokes and emerged on the other side.

The flat rock came up sooner than Melissa had remembered. She had planned to paddle out into the lake and observe it from a distance. But she rounded a bend and it was right there. At first, relief flooded her. Nobody in sight—just the bare gray rock gleaming in the hot sun. Then she spotted the blue canoe floating in the reeds. Before Melissa could turn around, someone waded out of the shade cast by the low boughs of a tree overhanging the water.

It was a girl in a red bathing suit, standing waist deep. She had long blond hair that hung down her back and a thin pointed face. She didn't look at all surprised to see Melissa. In fact, Melissa thought afterward, it was as if she had expected her.

When she spoke, her voice was firm and confident. "Do you come in peace or war?" she said.

"What?" said Melissa. Her cheeks turned hot with confusion.

The girl's light hazel eyes stared at Melissa steadily. "Are you friend or foe?"

Seven

The canoe drifted forward of its own will. Melissa hardly felt she could start to paddle backward, though it was what she wanted to do.

The girl hoisted herself onto the rock and sat on the smooth edge, dripping water, her legs dangling in the lake. She studied Melissa and then suddenly grinned. "I was just kidding," she said.

"I know," said Melissa quickly.

"I'm Alice May Hope," said the girl.

Melissa wasn't sure if that was meant to be said all together. Alice-May. "I'm Melissa."

"Do you have a nickname?"

"No." Sharlene was the only person who ever called her Mel.

"Me neither. I just like being called Alice."

So *not* Alice-May. Problem solved.

Melissa tried to think of something to say. "We just got here. We're staying in the Templetons' cabin."

"I know," said Alice. "I saw you come. I watched you through my binoculars. Your little brother is very cute. And your mother is beautiful."

Binoculars! Melissa felt uneasy. Had Alice been spying on them this morning too, while she was giving Cody his swimming lesson?

"You can get out of your canoe if you want, you know," said Alice. "I don't own this rock."

Melissa wasn't sure she wanted to. Alice seemed kind of strange. What was all that *Do you come in peace or war?* stuff about? But she looked around for somewhere to tie the canoe. Up against the bank was a submerged log with a long pointed branch that stuck up above the water. She was conscious of Alice watching her as she maneuvered the canoe beside it. Gripping both sides of the canoe, she managed to step out onto the log, which was slippery, and then onto the bank. She tied the bow rope to the branch and climbed onto the hot rock. She sat down beside Alice, her chest tightening with the familiar shyness.

She needn't have worried about finding things to say. Alice peppered her with questions, her eyes bright with curiosity. How long were they staying?

Where did they come from? What was her brother's name? How old was he? Where was her father?

Melissa struggled to answer everything. She kept the details about her father brief. He had disappeared years ago and Melissa didn't remember him. Cody had a different father, a guy called Mike who Melissa vaguely remembered as a tall man with a beard. Mike was two boyfriends before Darren.

It was flattering and scary at the same time to be the object of such interest. Alice volunteered only a tiny bit of information about herself. Her family had moved to the lake a year and a half ago. Her mother worked for a publishing company and flew back and forth to Vancouver a lot, and her father ran the ranch.

"Do you have any brothers or sisters?" asked Melissa.

Alice hesitated for a fraction of a second. Then she said, "I have one brother. His name is Austin and he's fifteen."

"Where do you go to school?"

"I don't. I'm homeschooled."

Melissa wasn't sure she had that right. "You mean you don't go to school at all?"

"I do it at home. Just since we moved to the ranch. My work comes in the mail and then I send stuff back. My mother is like my teacher," said Alice.

Melissa felt a pang of envy. If you didn't have to go to school, you wouldn't have to worry about being picked for a partner or having someone to walk around with at lunchtime. But Sharlene for a teacher? "I don't think I would like that," she said. "My mom would drive me crazy."

A slight frown crossed Alice's thin face. "My mom and I get along great," she said.

"Do you have to do work every day?" said Melissa.

"Of course. It's real school. But not *now*. It's summer holidays. And who wants to talk about school in the holidays? Do you like fantasy?"

"I'm not sure what you mean," said Melissa. She found it hard to keep up with Alice's questions. They bounced all over the place like corn popping.

"You know, books with battles against evil and quests and elves and dwarves and stuff like that. Books by authors like R.A. Salvatore and Robert Jordan. Like the Wheel of Time series."

Melissa had never heard of those authors. "I mostly read mysteries," she said. "I don't actually read that much. I don't really like it."

"You're kidding," said Alice. "That's so hard to believe. I love reading. My mom taught me to read when I was four."

Melissa prickled. "Not everyone is a reader," she said. She glanced around. "Were those your books here yesterday?"

Alice looked taken aback. So Alice *hadn't* seen her then. Melissa felt that this was a tiny victory. "Yeah, they were mine," said Alice after a moment.

"Are you reading them all at the same time?" said Melissa.

"I've already read them. I'm just reading bits over again for inspiration." Alice stretched her long legs out of the water. Her toenails were painted black. "I'm writing my own fantasy story. I come out here to work on it. I was just taking a break."

"Oh," said Melissa, unsure what to say.

"If I tell you what it's about, you won't tell anyone, will you? I don't want anyone to steal my idea."

"No," said Melissa. Who would she tell?

Alice launched into a long winding explanation of the story. It sounded very complicated. The main character was a girl called Elfrida. Her little brother was stolen by some fairies and a changeling left in his place.

Changelings, Alice explained, were creatures from the Invisible World who looked like humans but weren't. They were usually sick and didn't live long. Often they were very old, even though they looked like children. At the end of her story, there was going to be a big battle against the fairies to get Elfrida's real brother back.

How had Alice made all that up? Melissa had enough trouble coming up with any kind of idea during creative writing classes at school. "I thought fairies were supposed to be good," she ventured.

For a second, Alice looked annoyed, as if Melissa had criticized her. "Not *all* fairies. There are dark fairies too. I think the fairies in my story are going to be spriggans. I read about them on the Internet. Spriggans are grotesque. They can inflate themselves into monsters, so some people think they're the ghosts of old giants. They often kidnap children."

Alice sounded like she thought the stuff in her story really happened. Like Elfrida was a real person. Melissa tried to concentrate harder on what Alice was saying. "Do you think Elfrida is a good name?" said Alice. "Names are important in fantasies."

Melissa wasn't used to anyone asking her opinion. She was pretty sure most of the kids at school didn't even know she existed. "Sure," she said. "I like it."

She could feel Alice scrutinizing her. Her cheeks turned warm.

Then Alice stood up. "I believe you hail from a peaceable kingdom from over the mountains," she declared solemnly. "After much deliberation, I have made my decision. Come, I will take you to my stronghold."

Alice led Melissa along a rough narrow path that led right into the middle of the island. Melissa was glad she had worn her runners this time; the ground was littered with sharp sticks and scattered rocks. The trees were tall, with black trunks and straggly gray moss hanging from the branches. They grew close together, letting only a few rays of sunlight filter through high above the girls' heads.

Alice didn't say anything as they walked, and Melissa used the chance to unscramble her thoughts. She felt partly excited and partly nervous about meeting Alice. She was way friendlier than any of the girls at school, but it was embarrassing when she talked in that weird way. It was like she was trying to be a character in one of those fantasy books. There was no way Melissa was going to talk like that too. She decided the best thing to do would be to ignore it.

Suddenly the trees parted in front of them, opening into a small sunny clearing. Alice watched Melissa's face and then said triumphantly, "You can't see it, can you?"

Melissa shook her head, not sure exactly what she was looking for (What *was* a stronghold?), and Alice pointed up into the dense branches of a huge evergreen tree. "Up there."

Melissa stared high into the tree and spotted a circular wooden platform with a waist-high wall made of weathered gray boards, built right up against the massive trunk. "It's a tree house!" she said in surprise. "How did it get there?"

"My brother Austin built it last summer," said Alice. "He built it for me. Well, I helped too. It was a ton of work. We came every day until it was finished."

"But it looks so old," blurted Melissa.

There was a short silence. Then Alice said, "It *looks* old because we used old boards from a barn that fell down on the ranch. Dad said we could use them. Austin and I found this clearing when we were having a picnic one day."

An older brother who went on picnics with you and built you a tree house! "You're lucky," said Melissa.

"I know," said Alice. "I have the best brother in the world."

"Does he come over here a lot?" Melissa tried to make her voice sound casual but she knew she would be totally tongue-tied around a fifteen-year-old boy.

She held her breath until Alice said, "Well, not *right* now. He's helping my dad hay. He has to work all day. But *usually* he hangs out with me. He's my best friend."

It would be wonderful to have a best friend right in your own family, thought Melissa enviously. Then you wouldn't have to explain all the hard bits or try to hide things. She stared up at the tree house. "So how do you get up there?" she said. There were no branches low enough to climb.

"There's steps nailed on the trunk on the other side. We put them there so that enemies wouldn't see them. It was Austin's idea." Alice paused. "I'll let you come up, but only if you're sworn to secrecy."

"I swear," said Melissa.

Alice went first. The steps were made of thick boards. It was like climbing up the rungs of a ladder. There was a hole in the floor of the platform at the top. Alice pulled herself through and Melissa scrambled after her.

"Welcome to Dar Wynd," said Alice.

"Dar Wynd?"

Alice spread her arms. "This is Dar Wynd."

Melissa gazed around, impressed. "Wow."

It was like a little room with branches and blue sky for a ceiling. A sleeping bag with a plaid lining, unzipped and laid flat, covered the middle of the floor like a rug. Sheets of lined paper, some filled with writing, were scattered across the sleeping bag. The end of a red plastic binder poked out from under the papers. Lined up neatly along a board shelf were cans of fruit, beans and soup, a can opener, a plastic container full of water, a large round cookie tin with a lid, a bowl, a spoon and a mug. On another shelf was a row of books supported at each end by a large rock.

The bow that Melissa had seen at the flat rock leaned against the wall beside a pile of short sticks.

"What will you do if it rains?" said Melissa. "Your stuff will get ruined."

"It won't rain," said Alice confidently. "It's supposed to stay sunny for ages." She grinned. "But just in case…" She pointed to a stack of folded green garbage bags under the shelf with the books. "I can put everything in a garbage bag!"

"What does Dar Wynd mean?" asked Melissa.

"It doesn't mean anything. I just like the sound of it. It sounds like *wind* but I spell it W-y-n-d. I think the way words look is important. It's the name of the castle in my story, where Elfrida lives."

The girls sat on the sleeping bag. Alice gathered up her papers and tucked them inside the binder. Then she opened the round tin and held it out for Melissa. "Have a cookie. They're assorted. Mom bought them for me just for here. Usually she bakes cookies but she's working on a deadline right now."

Sharlene never baked cookies. She always said she was too dead on her feet to bake anything after cleaning up after schoolkids all day. Instead she bought the bulk boxes of cookies that never tasted as good as they looked and were often broken. Alice's family sounded perfect.

Alice filled a blue pottery mug with water. She took a sip and then handed it to Melissa. Melissa stared at the mug and felt her breath catch in her throat. It was identical to the mugs with the loons in the cabin.

"Did you get this from our cabin?" she said, then instantly wished she could take the words back. It sounded like she was accusing Alice of stealing.

Alice stared at her. Melissa felt her face go scarlet. "I mean, it's probably just a coincidence but we have some just like this."

Alice burst out laughing. "You should see your face," she said. "You look like you think I'm some kind of criminal."

"No, I don't," said Melissa, mortified.

"Yeah, I got it from the cabin," said Alice casually. "I guess you found the broken window."

Melissa nodded, shocked.

"It wasn't me that broke it," said Alice. "It was already broken. I just had to stick my hand through the hole and open the latch. And I just borrowed a bit of stuff. It's not a big deal."

Melissa felt a mix of horror and admiration. She'd have been terrified to do something like that; terrified of getting cut on the glass, terrified of being caught. Suddenly she remembered the silver bracelet with the letter *A* that was still in her pocket. She took it out. "I found this," she said. "On the dock."

"Oh, *thanks*!" said Alice. "I wondered where I dropped it." She took it from Melissa and slipped it on her wrist. She looked really pleased, and to Melissa's relief the difficult moment slipped away.

"You'll have to bring a mug for yourself next time," said Alice.

Next time. Was Alice going to share Dar Wynd? Melissa turned this idea over in her mind. Her life had been crowded with Cody, cluttered trailers and tiny apartments. In Dar Wynd there were no annoying little brothers and no embarrassing mothers.

Melissa was on her third cookie when she suddenly realized that Sharlene must be wondering what had happened to her. She stood up. "I think I better go."

Alice was silent while Melissa slid through the hole and climbed down the steps. Then she leaned over the wall and said, "Come back tomorrow."

Melissa hopped from the bottom rung onto the ground. Meeting Alice and going to the tree house were the most exciting things that had happened to her for a long time, but she didn't want Alice to think she could boss her around.

"I'll try," she said.

Eight

Sharlene had taped a paper on the wall that said *Flycatcher Lake Boggle Tournament*. She had drawn a line down the middle and written Melissa's name at the top of one side and her name on the other. Their games from yesterday were recorded. So far Melissa was winning.

Melissa ignored the paper all through supper. She read Cody two picturebooks to help him fall asleep. When she came back into the main room, Sharlene had lit the oil lamps and spread the game out on the table. She said, "Best out of five. You need to defend your title as champ so far."

She sounded so eager that Melissa gave in. They slid into the game quickly. Melissa was surprised to see how fast the time flew by until she was declared the winner at three games to two.

"You're killing me with those bonus points," said Sharlene. "*Slippery!* Eight letters! How could I see *slipper* and miss *slippery*?"

Melissa picked up a letter cube and turned it around in her fingers. "I met Alice Hope today," she said. "She was at the island."

Sharlene looked surprised. Then she said, "Really? That's great." She seemed so interested that Melissa immediately felt herself retreat. "What was she doing there?"

Melissa shrugged. "Nothing much. There's a big flat rock where you can sunbathe. She was just hanging out."

"What's she like?"

"Okay." When Alice had sworn Melissa to secrecy, Melissa was pretty sure she just meant Dar Wynd, but she quickly rejected the idea of telling Sharlene that Alice had taken the things from the cabin. Alice was right; it was really no big deal. After all, it wasn't anything *valuable*, but Sharlene probably wouldn't agree. Melissa dropped the cube into its hole and slid the tray into the box. She gathered up the papers and pencils.

"Just okay?" said Sharlene.

"She's nice." Alice was hard to explain. "She talks a lot. She's writing a fantasy story."

"A writer. That's neat," said Sharlene. "It will make a big difference for you to have a friend to do stuff with. Why don't you invite her over here? Maybe she could even come for supper."

Melissa sighed. It had been a huge mistake telling Sharlene. Alice's mother had an important job in Vancouver. What if Alice saw Sharlene's high school English course lying around? And Cody could be in one of his monster moods.

And besides, Melissa had an uneasy feeling that Sharlene wouldn't approve of Alice.

She frowned. "I might."

Cody lay on his back in the water, as rigid as a board, supported by Melissa's hands. He looked like a soldier, his arms clamped tight to his sides. Melissa had a vague memory of a swimming instructor telling her to be a starfish.

"Pretend you're a starfish," said Melissa. She slid one hand out and tried to loosen Cody's grip.

He screwed up his face and gasped, "Don't let go!"

Melissa held him for a few more seconds.

Then Cody sputtered "No more!" and struggled to put his feet down.

"Well done, Cody!" called Sharlene from the porch when the little boy was upright again.

"He won't put his face in the water," said Melissa. "How can he learn to swim if he won't put his face in the water?"

"I don't want to!" roared Cody. He tipped his head sideways and peered under the dock. "I see fish!"

"Rome wasn't built in a week," said Sharlene, laughing. "How about a lemonade-and-cookie break?" She put her book down on the arm of her chair. "I'll bring it out. I need to move. I don't know how you do school all day. It's only eleven o'clock and my head feels like it's full of cotton."

Melissa swam on her back out into the flat blue lake, one eye on Cody. There was a warm layer on top, but when she let her feet dangle down, they slid into coolness. Something slippery and weedlike slapped at her legs. She pretended that a sea monster was after her and swam in quick strong strokes to the shore.

Sharlene was back with a tray loaded with a jug, cups and a package of cookies. Melissa sat dripping on the edge of the porch, the sun warming her back, and Cody climbed into a lawn chair. How could she be so hungry, she wondered, devouring her first cookie in two bites, when they had just had bacon and eggs not that long ago?

"Do you hear something?" said Sharlene.

Melissa stopped mid chew and listened. An engine—a car engine—was steadily getting louder. She got up and walked to the end of the porch so she could see the road.

"Someone's coming," she said. "It's a red truck."

The truck bounced over the ruts and stopped beside the cabin. It was covered in dust and had an aluminum boat strapped to the roof. The front doors opened and two men climbed out. Melissa felt a stab of apprehension as she recognized the man with the beard and the man with the dragon tattoo from the store.

They strolled around to the front of the cabin. They were both holding cans of beer. "So this is where you're hiding," said the man with the tattoo. "I'm Matt, and this here is my buddy Tyler."

Sharlene didn't get up. "Can I help you?" she said.

Matt grinned. "Hey, this looks like happy hour. Can I offer you a beer? We got a cooler full in the truck."

"No, thank you," said Sharlene. "We'll stick with our lemonade."

Tyler had wandered down to the edge of the lake. He turned around and said, "This would be a good place to launch our boat."

"I'd rather you didn't," said Sharlene. "This is actually private property." She was smiling but there was an edge in her voice.

Matt raised both hands as if in defense. "Whoa there, lady, this is not exactly a friendly reception. What's your problem? Have a beer. Lighten up a little."

Cody stared at the man, mouth open. Melissa's heart raced. She had no idea what her mother was going to do.

Sharlene stood up. "I think you'd better go."

Tyler walked back toward the truck. "Let's get out of here, Matt." He sounded bored. "I bet the fishing's lousy in this lake anyway."

Matt looked Sharlene up and down. Then he tipped his beer can and said, "A pleasure to meet you, ma'am."

He winked at Cody. "See you, kid."

Melissa held her breath. Doors slammed and the truck disappeared back the way it had come.

They were gone. Nothing bad had happened.

"Do you think they'll come back?" said Melissa shakily.

"No," said Sharlene. She smiled at Melissa. "Why should they? There's nothing to come back for."

More than anything, Melissa wanted to believe her mother. But she could feel the back of her neck prickle.

Nine

*E*lfrida galloped through the green valley on her black stallion Nightshadow, her long golden hair blowing in the wind. The castle where she lived stood at one end of the valley. It was called Dar Wynd and had been owned by generations of her family for six hundred years. She stopped her horse and admired the tall towers that reached into the blue sky. Then she spurred Nightshadow on. She had promised to take her little brother, Tristan, for a ride this afternoon. He was four years old and big enough to sit in front of her on the powerful stallion. She smiled when she thought of her beloved brother Tristan. He was a strong little boy with red cheeks, and he laughed all the time.

Elfrida left Nightshadow with a groom. "Give him some oats," she said, "but do not unbridle him. Tristan and I are going riding together."

She clattered in her riding boots across the stone floor of the entrance hall. Milly, one of the servants, rushed past her with a basin of water. She had a frightened look on her face. She had been crying.

"Milly, what is it?" demanded Elfrida. "Where are you going with that water?"

"To Master Tristan's room," said Milly.

"Why? What is wrong with Master Tristan?"

"He has taken poorly. Very poorly. Why, I have never seen the likes of such a thing."

Elfrida's heart pounded with fright. "What do you mean?"

"Nurse was making him a hot drink. She left him playing with his wooden blocks. When she came back, he was lying on the floor crying as if he had a broken heart. She called your mama at once." Milly sniffed and tears started to pour down her face again. "They have put him to bed. There is something dreadfully wrong with him."

Elfrida ran up the stairs ahead of Milly. She raced down the hallway to Tristan's room. She stood outside the door, her heart beating fast. Then she went in the room.

Elfrida's mother, Amarantha, was sitting beside Tristan's bed. She was wearing a long purple robe.

Her cheeks were white. "Hush," she said. "I have only just got him to go to sleep."

Elfrida stood beside the bed, trembling, and stared at her little brother. A gasp of shock burst out of her. Instead of her brother's chubby pink face, she saw thin, sunken white cheeks like the face of an old man. His hair was like limp straw, and Elfrida was surprised to see how long it looked. It almost touched his shoulders.

Behind her the nurse whispered, "It is a sad day in the house of Dar Wynd."

Amarantha sent for the old lady, Dame Bridget, who lived in the village and was known all over the land for her great wisdom. She brought a bag of healing herbs. She examined the sick boy and then shook her head.

"Was he crying when you found him?" she asked.

"Yes, he was," said Nurse. "Louder than I have ever heard him cry. Tristan is usually such a happy little boy."

"Amarantha, this is not Tristan," said Dame Bridget sadly. "I have seen your little boy in the village and I know him. I fear Dar Wynd has been visited by the fairies. They have taken your healthy Tristan and left you one of theirs to raise. This boy is a changeling. He is not human. There is no doubt in my mind."

"That cannot be!" shrieked Amarantha. "It is true he looks different, but it is because of this strange illness he has."

Dame Bridget pulled back some of the limp hair and revealed the boy's long pointed ears.

Everybody gasped.

A changeling!

Amarantha's wails of grief sent shivers up and down Elfrida's spine. "I will find my brother Tristan," Elfrida vowed to herself. "I will bring him home."

"That's as far as I want you to read," said Alice. She was sitting cross-legged on the sleeping bag, her sharp eyes on Melissa. "I still need to work on the next part."

Melissa put the papers down. "It's really good. It sounds just like a real book. I could never have thought of all that."

Alice shrugged. "It's okay," she said, but she looked pleased. She stood up. "I've decided you can help with the arrows."

"What arrows?" said Melissa.

"For Elfrida's bow. Austin helped me make the bow but he's too busy to make arrows. He'd *like* to help but he can't. I've got all the sticks. They need to be peeled and then sharpened into a point. I've brought two knives."

The tree house was cool and shady. Melissa leaned her back against the wall. She held a stick firmly in her hand and tried a few experimental scrapes with the edge of the knife. The bark held tight and she pressed the blade harder into the wood. A long strip peeled back, revealing the pale green wood hidden underneath.

Thin slices of bark drifted over her lap. Melissa felt herself relax as she listened to Alice describe in detail the movie she and Austin had watched the night before. It was based on a book called *The Lion, the Witch and the Wardrobe,* and Alice said it had given her lots of ideas for her story. "I'd like to put a faun in my story, but I don't know if that would be copying." She grunted as her knife skittered across her stick. "Austin made popcorn while we were watching the movie and we had a popcorn fight. It was so much fun."

She examined her stick critically and then looked at Melissa's. "Yours looks better than mine. Mine's all ragged."

Melissa flushed with pleasure. The secret was to ease the knife gently into the bark. Alice was going too fast but Melissa didn't want to tell her that. "Do you think the bow will work?" she said.

"It doesn't really matter," said Alice. "It's for inspiration to help me write. I've decided that Elfrida's older brother, Warwick, has been giving her secret lessons in shooting a bow and arrow. They have to be secret because she's a girl. She's going to need weapons to battle the fairies."

Melissa ran her fingers along the smooth inner wood. She was almost finished. "Are the fairies still going to be...whatever you called them?"

"Spriggans? I think so." Alice sounded distracted. "By the way, what happened to your hand?"

Melissa felt like she had been slammed in the chest.

"You don't mind me asking, do you? I've been kind of wondering."

"No." Heat rushed into Melissa's face. She was angry that she had let herself be caught off guard. What version to give Alice? The edited one, with all the bad parts snipped out. The rest was none of her business. "We had a fire. It started in the kitchen. Some oil spilled on me." Melissa's voice shook. She bit down on her lip. *One, two, three, breathe.*

"Wow," said Alice. "That must have hurt like crazy."

Melissa didn't say anything.

"Was, like, the whole kitchen on fire?"

Try the whole trailer. "Yeah," said Melissa.

"Wow."

Alice was gaping at her. Melissa waited for the look of embarrassment or, even worse, pity. But Alice's gaze was open and curious. "You'd be able to write an amazing story about a fire, having actually experienced one."

"Why would I want to write a story about a fire?" said Melissa tightly. She wished Alice would stop staring at her. "I hate writing."

"God, that must have hurt," persisted Alice. "What exactly happened?"

"I don't really want to talk about it." Melissa could hear the coldness in her voice and changed the subject. "Do you feel like going for a swim?"

"Right now?" said Alice. "Sure." She stood up and brushed bits of bark off her legs. "It's not like we have to make all the arrows today."

She picked up a towel that was crumpled in a heap on the floor. She seemed to have forgotten all about Melissa's hand. "And then afterward, there's something I want to show you."

Ten

"We'll take my canoe," said Alice.

"Where are we going?" said Melissa. She was lying on her stomach on the flat rock, drying off in the hot sun. The swim had been amazing, the water like cool silk. Now she felt like a lizard, unable to move.

"Get your paddle," said Alice.

Melissa reluctantly sat up. "Where are we going?" she repeated.

"You'll see," said Alice mysteriously.

Melissa retrieved her paddle and climbed into the bow of Alice's canoe. Alice scrambled into the back and untied the rope. It was much easier to paddle a canoe with two people, Melissa quickly discovered. She was amazed at how fast they skimmed across the still water.

They paddled straight across the lake to the opposite shore. It was very rocky on this side of the lake, and the forest went straight uphill from the edge of the water. There were no lily pads or reeds, just deep green water. Melissa rested her paddle for a moment and stuck her hand in the lake. The water ran in silver lines between her fingers.

"It's along here a little ways," said Alice. "Just around that point."

They glided in and out of shade, rapidly approaching the point, which was covered with dead trees. They paddled past it, into the mouth of a narrow bay shaded by the steep forested hillside that circled it. At the end of the bay was a high cliff with an exposed sunny outcropping of rock at the top.

Three ducks, their peace disturbed, splashed across the smooth water and flew into the sky. A dragonfly hovered near the canoe, its wings glistening. Alice let her paddle drag. "This is it. D'you think anyone has ever jumped off that cliff?"

Melissa stared up at the cliff. "No," she said, though she had a feeling that Alice was going to tell her that she was wrong.

"My brother Austin did. Last summer. He's not afraid to do anything." Alice dug her paddle into the water. "If we get right up close, there's a place where we can land. There's a trail to the top."

The girls paddled into the end of the bay until the cliff loomed over their heads. They tied the canoe to a dead tree and scrambled onto the shore. A steep trail zigzagged up between the trees. The ground, carpeted in pine needles, was hot on their bare feet as they climbed. In a few minutes they emerged onto the open rocky outcropping, breathing hard.

The dark narrow bay lay below them, as still as a piece of glass. Alice walked right to the edge of the cliff, but Melissa hung back. Heights had always given her a sick feeling. She remembered once climbing all the way to the top of the ladder on the high diving board at the pool in Huntley and then being embarrassed when everyone had to get off the ladder so she could go back down. The lifeguard had frowned at her and some boys had jeered.

"He jumped right from here," reported Alice. She looked over her shoulder at Melissa. Her eyes gleamed with excitement. "He said it felt fantastic. He said it didn't hurt at all when he landed."

"Oh," said Melissa.

"Are you afraid to stand on the edge?" said Alice.

"Not really," said Melissa. "I just don't want to, that's all."

"What about jumping? Would you be afraid to jump?"

"I don't know," said Melissa. "It's just not my thing."

Alice peered over the edge one last time and then walked back to Melissa. "This is my plan," she said.

Melissa felt a tickle of apprehension run up her back.

"We agree to jump. Both of us."

"I don't want to," said Melissa quickly.

"I don't mean now. We have to psych ourselves up for this. We'll make a pact. We'll solemnly swear to jump in one week."

"No," said Melissa.

"I thought you were in on this," said Alice.

"In on what?" said Melissa weakly.

"This whole thing. Being part of Dar Wynd. Elfrida is brave. She'd do it."

You're the one who's pretending to be Elfrida, not me, thought Melissa. Alice's stare made her uncomfortable.

"We need some kind of test of bravery," Alice persisted. "And it's not like it's even dangerous or anything. Austin's done it tons of times."

That's not how she had made it sound before, thought Melissa. She had pictured Austin jumping once, that was all. Maybe he had just been lucky. "I'd never be able to do it," she said.

There was a short silence. Then Alice said frostily, "Okay, I'll do it by myself. And I'll have to think about all this. You coming to Dar Wynd, I mean. It's not going to work if you won't do stuff."

What kind of stuff? For a second, Melissa pictured

Alice climbing in the window of their cabin. Was that the kind of stuff she meant? Melissa felt miserable as she followed Alice back down the trail to the canoe. She scrambled in her mind for a way to repair the rift that had sprung up between them. Alice had said they would jump in one week. Melissa could always pretend to be part of the pact and then at the very end say she had changed her mind.

Melissa sucked in her breath. "Okay, I'll do it," she said slowly.

Alice spun around, a wide smile lighting up her face. "We'll prick our fingers with the knife when we get back to Dar Wynd. This is going to be great. I'm so glad you came here, Melissa!"

Melissa flushed. No one had ever said anything like that to her before. She felt guilty about deceiving Alice, but it was worth it if she got to keep her for a friend.

"May the gods witness this deed," whispered Alice. "We take the oath to jump from the High Cliff on the eleventh of August. We seal this pact with the blood cast this day at the stronghold of Dar Wynd."

Melissa studied the pinprick of deep red blood that sprang up on the tip of her thumb. She glanced up at Alice's pale face, pinched with excitement, and shivered.

Eleven

When Melissa got back to the cabin, there was a note on the table from her mother.

Cody and I have gone to the store. Keeping ice is a full-time job. NO SWIMMING BY YOURSELF!!! Love Mom

Melissa got out her sketchbook and pencils and settled herself on the porch. She doodled for a few minutes while she decided what to draw. Her mind drifted to the pact that she and Alice had made. It had been dumb, really, pricking their fingers with the knife. The kind of thing little kids did. But Alice had taken it so seriously.

There was no way Melissa was going to jump off that cliff. She knew that about herself. It made her sick just thinking about it. She shrugged away the worrisome thought and started to sketch the dock with the red canoe tied at the end. She was just finishing shading the weathered boards when Cody and Sharlene returned.

"Mail! Can you believe it?" said Sharlene. She handed Melissa an envelope. "I feel like a local. It's from Jill. She sent it General Delivery. It's to all of us. You can open it if you like. And I met Bonnie Hill from the guest ranch. She was picking up her mail. She's coming over for iced tea in a few minutes."

Sharlene attracts people the way honey attracts bears, thought Melissa. Pretty soon she would be friends with the whole neighborhood. Sharlene disappeared inside the cabin with Cody, who had spilt pop all down his shirt and needed a clean one. Melissa examined the French stamps for a second and then slit open the envelope and took out a folded piece of paper.

"What does she say?" Sharlene called through the open door.

"Mmmm…she's having a great time. She's been to the Louvre and she says I would love the art there. And she went up the Eiffel Tower but she didn't walk. She took the elevator." Melissa skimmed over the rest quickly. "The life jackets are in the shed, which we already know, and—"

Melissa frowned. She read the next part twice.

Melissa, don't forget to check out the island. There's a neat tree fort in the middle that my sons built. They used to play "Marooned on a Desert Island."

Sharlene came out carrying a tray of glasses and a jug of iced tea just as a brown pickup truck stopped beside the cabin. Cody trailed at her heels with his thumb in his mouth. Melissa folded the paper and put it back in the envelope. "You can read it yourself," she said.

Her mind whirled with confusion. Jill's *sons* had built the tree house? So why had Alice said that it was her and Austin? There was no way Jill Templeton would *lie*. So it must have been Alice who had lied. Why?

A short freckled woman wearing jeans and dusty cowboy boots stepped out of the truck, and Melissa pulled her thoughts away from the letter. Sharlene introduced Bonnie Hill, who admired Melissa's drawing and let Cody show her the fish under the dock before everyone settled down in lawn chairs with glasses of iced tea.

Melissa closed her eyes and listened while Sharlene asked Bonnie a million questions about running a guest ranch. No wonder everyone liked Sharlene. She's really *interested* in people, thought Melissa almost grudgingly.

But not us, she reminded herself. She remembered all those years when Sharlene was too busy with her boyfriends, and Melissa had struggled to look out for Cody. She shifted in her chair. The counselor had told her to focus on the times when Sharlene had tried to be a good mother. Melissa had dug into her memory and come up with the time when she was six and had the chicken pox and Sharlene had made special meals and played cards with her. It had been a perfect week and Melissa had actually been sorry when the doctor said she was well enough to go back to school. There were other scattered memories: Sharlene's once-in-a-lifetime effort at baking lumpy green cupcakes that none of the kids would eat for a school St. Patrick's Day party; Sharlene sitting in the front row of the gym at a Christmas concert, taking flash pictures and laughing too loudly. It was the drinking that had messed her mother up, the counselor had explained to Melissa. Her intentions had always been good.

"Melissa?" said Sharlene, and Melissa realized that Bonnie was talking to her. "Pardon," she said quickly, focusing on Bonnie's smiling face.

"You seem like a very talented artist. I hope you're going to put some of your drawings in the fair."

Had Sharlene prompted her to say that? Probably. Melissa's pictures were private. Melissa shrugged.

She ignored the frown on her mother's face and stood up. "I'm going to go inside. It's too hot out here."

❧

"That was extremely rude," said Sharlene. She stood in the doorway of Melissa's bedroom.

Melissa was lying on her stomach on her bed. She had been picking away in her brain at Alice's lie. Why had she said that she and Austin had built the tree house when it wasn't true? Had she lied about other stuff too? Melissa rolled onto her back and studied the ceiling. "What do you mean?"

"You know exactly what I mean. Bonnie was trying to be friendly about your drawing and you didn't even have the decency to answer her."

"I don't want everyone to keep pestering me about putting my drawings in the fair." Melissa could hear how weak that sounded. But she didn't have the courage to tell Sharlene what was really bothering her. She didn't exactly understand it herself but it had something to do with hearing her mother laugh and chat with Bonnie, pretending that they were a normal family when they weren't.

What would Bonnie think if she knew what the real Sharlene was like? Melissa flopped back on her stomach and buried her face in her pillow.

"I'd appreciate some help with supper," said Sharlene tightly. "I got some corn at the store that you can shuck. And after supper you and Cody and I are going fishing."

Not, would you *like* to go fishing? Not, maybe you have something else you'd rather do. Melissa sighed. The trouble was, there *was* nothing else to do here. The only good thing that had happened so far was Alice and Dar Wynd. And now her feelings about that were mixed up with Alice's lie and jumping off that stupid cliff. Melissa closed her eyes until she heard the angry banging of pots from the other room that told her that Sharlene had left her alone.

Melissa sat in the bow of the canoe, Cody in the middle and Sharlene in the stern. Cody had refused to wear a life jacket unless Melissa did too. Melissa's jacket was too small and bumped her chin. It didn't improve her mood.

They paddled into a small deep cove partway up the lake and let themselves drift. Sharlene had brought a fishing rod along, which she had fiddled with after supper, unscrambling the line, attaching something she called a sinker, which she found in a tackle box in the shed. Melissa had pretended to be uninterested but inside she was impressed. Her mother acted like she knew what she was doing.

Sharlene baited the hook with a shrimp, dropped the line over the side of the canoe and handed the rod to Cody. Cody stared at the water, his mouth open. "If you feel something jiggle, let me know," said Sharlene. Melissa stretched her legs out and closed her eyes. There was no sound here, not even a bird call. She thought of the apartment, where you could always hear someone's TV or people arguing in the hallways or the backfire of a truck.

Cody had three false alarms. The first two times Sharlene pulled in the line there was nothing on the hook except the shriveled-up pale pink shrimp. The third time there was a mass of gnarled green weed that looked like a nest.

"We're drifting too close to shore," said Sharlene. "How about we paddle and let Cody troll the line behind us?"

Melissa studied the shore as they paddled up the lake. Mostly it was dense forest, with tall dark trees that grew right up to the edge of the water, but in a few places there were grassy clearings sprinkled with purple and yellow wild flowers.

After a while, Cody announced that he didn't want to fish anymore. Sharlene reeled in the line and laid the fishing rod carefully in the bottom of the canoe. "We'll try worms tomorrow."

"I want to go back," said Cody.

"Not yet," said Sharlene. "It can't be much farther to the end of the lake. Pretend you're an explorer."

Cody hunched over and jammed his thumb in his mouth. Melissa was glad that for once Sharlene hadn't given in to her brother's demands. Now that they were out here, she had to admit she was enjoying herself. It was satisfying to feel the canoe surge forward each time she pulled the paddle through the still water.

"You're good in a canoe, Mel," said Sharlene suddenly. "You make very even strokes. I think we make a great team. When your Aunty Eleanor and I used to take our grandpa's canoe out, we argued steadily about who was paddling the hardest." Sharlene chuckled. "Once we got in a down-and-out fight and tipped the canoe right over!"

Melissa couldn't help grinning. She found it impossible to imagine Sharlene and her sister Eleanor as kids, canoeing on some lake that might have been a bit like this. Melissa didn't know her aunt very well, and the few times they got together, she always had the feeling that Aunty Eleanor disapproved of Sharlene.

She examined the compliment her mother had given her and imagined casually telling the kids at school that she had spent the summer canoeing.

"Oh my," said Sharlene suddenly in a low voice. "Keep quiet and look over to the right."

A sleek black and white bird drifted on the smooth water. It opened its bill and gave a long quavering cry.

"A loon," whispered Sharlene. "It's calling its mate."

Melissa scanned the lake and spotted another loon. "There it is!" she said, pointing. "Way over there."

The loons called back and forth. Goose bumps prickled Melissa's back. The sound was beautiful and sad at the same time.

For a long time they let the canoe drift while they watched the loons. Finally the birds dove and reappeared far in the distance. Melissa and Sharlene picked up their paddles. The canoe glided around a point of land that jutted into the water. "Look, Cody," said Sharlene. "Somebody lives here."

Cody looked up long enough to decide that it wasn't at all interesting and began to whine, "I want to go back. I want to go back."

"This must be the Hopes' ranch," said Sharlene.

Melissa's heart gave a jump. Rippling green fields stretched back from the lake. A tractor was parked in the middle of one field and a swath of mowed grass stretched like a ribbon behind it. The field next to it had been cut and was dotted with huge round bales of hay. A log house, the fading sunlight glinting off the dark windows, faced the lake, and a barn and several outbuildings were scattered behind. A long dock in front of the house was bare except for the blue canoe and an aluminum boat tied to the end.

Melissa thought of the clutter of lawn chairs, beach towels and Cody's toys that had spread across the grass and onto the dock in front of their cabin. Sharlene must have been thinking the same thing for she said, "It looks kind of lonely here."

Sharlene and Melissa rested their paddles and the canoe drifted toward the house. "Maybe we better go back," said Melissa quickly. Her heart raced in her chest. She was terrified that Alice would think she was spying on her.

At that moment a tall thin boy walked through a door onto the front porch of the house. He was wearing baggy blue jeans and a gray T-shirt with the arms cut off. His black hair was long and fell over one side of his face. He stopped and stared out at them, and Melissa's face flushed. "Come on," she urged. "It looks like we're being nosy."

"Nonsense," said Sharlene. She waved at the boy. "Hello!" she called out.

The boy stared a moment longer but made no sign that he had heard Sharlene. Then he wheeled around and disappeared back inside the house, slamming the door.

"See!" said Melissa, mortified. Was Alice watching them too, from one of the windows? She dug her paddle into the water and swung the canoe around.

Sharlene seemed bemused rather than upset by what had happened. "He certainly wasn't very neighborly," she said. "Although your friend Alice sounds like a nice girl. I'll ask Marge more about the family next time I'm at the store."

"It's none of our business," said Melissa firmly. The magic had gone out of the evening. It was harder to paddle back; a small breeze had kicked up and the water had roughened and was pushing against the bow of the canoe. Melissa thought about the boy on the porch. It must have been Austin. Alice made Austin sound like so much fun, but he didn't look like a boy who would have popcorn fights and take his sister on picnics. He looked like a boy who wanted to be left alone.

Twelve

The next day, Cody still refused to go any deeper in the lake than his waist. He hugged his chest and watched Melissa walk on her hands in the shallow water, her legs floating behind her. "I'm a crocodile," said Melissa. She bumped her head against Cody's legs and he scrambled back onto dry ground and stuck his thumb in his mouth.

"There's something on your leg," said Melissa, staring at a dark blob stuck to Cody's ankle. "It's a weird kind of worm."

Cody stared at the thing that stretched across his ankle. It looked like a long thin smear of black mud. He screamed.

Melissa stood up, water streaming from her shoulders and hair, and waded out of the lake. She brushed the worm thing with her fingers but it was stuck tight to Cody's skin.

Cody screamed harder.

"Whatever is the matter?" said Sharlene from the porch. She had been sitting in the shade, reading a battered paperback copy of *Hamlet*.

"There's some kind of worm thing on his leg," said Melissa.

"Let me see," said Sharlene, and Cody raced to her. He hopped up and down, hysterical. "It's a leech, not a worm," said Sharlene calmly.

"Oh, yuck," said Melissa. Cody burst into tears.

Sharlene disappeared inside the cabin and came back with a box of salt. She sprinkled salt on the leech and then peeled it off Cody's leg and flung it into the bushes. "It's no big deal. We had them all the time at Grandpa's cabin. Salt is the best way to get them off."

Cody's sobs had turned into hiccups. Sharlene wrapped him in a big striped beach towel and cuddled him on her lap. For once he didn't pull away but snuggled deeper into her chest. Sharlene kissed the top of his rumpled blond hair and then leaned back in her chair and closed her eyes.

Melissa studied her mother's face for a moment. Campstoves, J strokes, fishing rods and now leeches. What else did Sharlene know? If Melissa were drawing a picture of her mother, the lines wouldn't be clear anymore. They would be smudged, like when she shaded the logs on the log cabin.

Sharlene made bannock for lunch. She had found an old wilderness cookbook in the back of a cupboard and had announced with enthusiasm that they had all the necessary ingredients.

Melissa helped. She had never heard of bannock, but according to Sharlene it was kind of like a wilderness fried bread that First Nations people made.

"Two and a half cups of flour," read Sharlene. "We don't have a measuring cup but we can use a mug. We'll estimate."

Melissa measured the flour into a bowl and then stirred in four teaspoons of baking powder. "What's lard?" she said, peering at the recipe.

"Something margarine-like," said Sharlene. She dolloped three spoonfuls of soft margarine into the bowl. "Mix it in with your fingers until it's kind of crumbly."

"Did you do this at your grandpa's cabin?" said Melissa as she sifted her fingers through the mixture.

"Nope. First time," said Sharlene.

Melissa added water to make dough. Soon, round mounds of the dough were frying to a golden brown in a black cast-iron pan on the campstove.

"Some people cook bannock on a stick over a campfire," said Sharlene. "They kind of wrap it around like a snake. I don't know how I know that but I do. If the campfire ban lifts, we could try it."

Melissa pondered that information, wondering how you would keep the stick from burning up. They ate the bannock with margarine, which melted into little rivers, and raspberry jam.

"Can we have this for supper too?" said Cody, jam dripping on his chin.

"We can have it every day," said Sharlene comfortably.

"I thought you weren't coming." Alice's voice was flat and her gray eyes cold.

Melissa scrambled off the top of the ladder into the tree fort. She didn't want to explain that after they had cleaned up from the bannock, she and Sharlene had played six games of Boggle while Cody slept, belly full, jam-smeared and sun-tired, on the couch. "Sorry. I had to look after Cody longer than usual."

She wondered apprehensively if Alice was going to mention seeing them paddle past her house the night before. She couldn't get the picture out of her head of the tall dark boy with the angry face. "What's Austin doing today?" she said, trying to make her voice sound casual.

Alice frowned. Her sharp eyes studied Melissa for a moment. Then she said, "They're still haying. He's very busy, but he says he's coming to Dar Wynd as soon as he has time. He's very interested in what we're doing here and he wants to read my story."

Alice picked up a few sheets of paper covered in handwriting and said, "I've been working on this all morning. It's ready for you to read."

Melissa leaned back against the wall of the fort. She cast her mind over what had happened in the first part of the story—Elfrida's little brother, Tristan, had been stolen and a changeling left in his place, and Elfrida had vowed to get him back. She started to read, conscious of Alice's eyes watching her intently.

"Take him away! I cannot bear to look at him," wailed Elfrida's mother, Amarantha. "And make him stop crying. Oh, my poor baby, Tristan! Where are you?"

The maid carried the changeling from the room. The sick-looking boy stared at Elfrida as they left, and she shivered at the strange knowing look in his eyes.

There was a knock at the chamber door and Amarantha called out, "Come in."

It was Warwick, Elfrida's eighteen-year-old brother. He was walking with crutches, and one leg was bound tightly to a wooden splint. Two days ago he had been thrown from a young colt while he was training it and had broken his leg.

Warwick's face was pale. "Mama, I fear this may be all my fault."

Elfrida stared at him. "What do you mean?" said Amarantha.

"Three days ago I stopped at the Roaring Boar with some friends. There were some strangers in the tavern. A very rowdy group of little men with peculiar clothes and rough manners. They kept their hoods on and stayed out of the light." Warwick sighed. "I believe now that they were not men at all but spriggans!"

Elfrida gasped and Amarantha gave a little cry. Elfrida had heard stories of spriggans, the name given to the dark and dangerous fairies who lived in the ancient ruins of castles. They did terrible things to people who offended them, including sending storms to ruin their crops and stealing their children and leaving one of their own in its place.

"The leader of the group challenged anyone in the tavern to an arm wrestle, and I took up the challenge for a lark," said Warwick. "I beat him easily. He was no match at all! I flipped him right over onto the floor and caused everyone in the tavern to roar with laughter."

Amarantha was staring at Warwick in horror.

"It was foolish, Mama," admitted Warwick. "If I had known they were spriggans, I'd have left them alone."

"And then what happened?" interrupted Elfrida.

"He vowed revenge," whispered Warwick. "Then he and his companions left the tavern. Little did I know what they were plotting! They have taken Tristan! I would go after them but I cannot do a thing while I am a cripple on crutches!" His voice was bitter.

Melissa stopped reading. "What's going to happen to the changeling?" she said. "I mean, if Elfrida gets Tristan back. Will the changeling die?"

"He won't *die*," said Alice. "Elfrida will rescue Tristan and then the changeling will go back to the spriggans where he belongs."

"I feel kind of sorry for him," said Melissa.

"The changeling is *wicked*," said Alice. She sounded annoyed. "He's a spriggan. He's pretending to be Tristan. I don't think you get this. Don't you want the real Tristan back?"

For a second, Melissa was confused. Alice was sounding again as if the characters in her story really existed. "I do get it," she said finally. "I just said I felt sorry for the changeling, that's all."

Melissa turned back to the paper and kept reading.

No one noticed when Elfrida slipped from the room. She hurried to get her cloak and left the castle. She had a plan. She would go to the Roaring Boar at once. Someone must have talked to the spriggans. Someone must know where they had gone.

Elfrida ran through the shadowy streets to the Roaring Boar. The sign hanging over the door creaked in the wind. Elfrida opened the door cautiously and went inside. She wished she had worn one of her older capes so she wouldn't stand out so much.

The tavern was almost empty. A man with a round face was polishing tankards at the counter. Two rough-looking men sitting at a table stared at Elfrida and one of them gave a low whistle.

Elfrida took a big breath. "I am trying to get some information about a group of men who were here three nights ago. One of them had an arm wrestle with a gentleman."

The man put down his rag. "We don't get a lot of gentlemen in here. I remember the incident well.

The men were troublemakers. Not from these parts. I was glad to see the end of them. I don't need trouble in my tavern."

"Do you know where they went?"

"No idea."

Elfrida's eyes stung with disappointment. Then she noticed a shadow move in the corner of the tavern. A figure in a long hooded coat was sitting alone on a bench. "Come and talk to me," said a quavery voice.

Elfrida sat on the bench beside the figure. A withered hand pulled back the hood and Elfrida glimpsed a wrinkled face with bright brown eyes. It was an old woman!

"I'm Mareea," said the woman. She let the hood fall back over her face. "Why are you asking about spriggans?"

A chill ran down Elfrida's spine. Warwick was right! The rowdy strangers were not of this world at all but from the world of dark fairies! "They have taken my little brother and left a sick changeling in his place," she said. "I need to know where they have gone. I must get my brother back! Please, I beg you to tell me if you know."

For a long time, Mareea didn't speak. Finally she said, "I overheard them speak of the Dark Valley. That is a long ride from here through dangerous territory." The hood slipped farther back and Elfrida saw a greedy gleam in the old woman's eyes. "If you make it worth *my while, I will take you to the pass above the valley. No farther."*

"I can pay you ten silver coins," said Elfrida. It was all the money she had saved.

Mareea sighed. "I suppose that will do. We will leave at midnight. I will need something to ride. My old legs do not take me very far these days."

Elfrida thought quickly. She would ride Night-shadow and she would bring Willow, her old pony, for Mareea.

Mareea reached out her gnarled hand and touched a lock of Elfrida's long golden hair. "It would be safer to travel as a boy," she muttered.

Melissa looked up. "Elfrida's going to cut her hair!" she guessed.

"She has no choice." Alice spoke quickly. "That's the next part I have to write. I've thought about it a lot. It would be a hard thing to do because in those days girls didn't have short hair. But Elfrida would do anything to get her brother back."

"Did they have scissors then?" said Melissa.

"I don't know," said Alice. "But I think Elfrida will use a knife. It's more interesting that way." She pushed her hands through her long hair and let it fall around her shoulders. "I have to do it too," she said quietly.

"What? Cut your hair?" gasped Melissa.

"It will help me understand Elfrida's character better," said Alice. A strange sort of urgency seemed to have gripped her. "I'm going to do it now. Before I lose my nerve."

"How much are you going to cut off?" said Melissa, astounded. Alice's hair hung in a fine sheet halfway down her back.

Alice hesitated. "Not as much as Elfrida has to. I'm just trying to get the feeling. So I can write about it."

She's serious, thought Melissa as Alice picked up one of the knives they had used for the arrows. Alice separated her hair behind her neck and pulled one section forward. She held it in front of her. "Okay, here goes," she muttered.

Melissa held her breath, her eyes riveted on Alice. The knife made a rasping sound as Alice sawed back and forth against the swath of glistening hair. "It's too slippery," she complained. "The knife won't go through."

"You could put your hair in two braids," suggested Melissa. "And then just cut off the end. It might be easier."

She was half joking. But Alice gave her a specu-lative look. "Good idea," she said. While Melissa watched in disbelief, Alice twisted her hair deftly into two long braids. She gripped one braid just above her shoulder and hacked at it with the knife.

"Oh!" Alice gasped as the piece of braid broke off. Her hair sprang loose, ending in a ragged line.

"What does it look like?" Alice put her hand up and touched the ends. Her eyes were bright with triumph. "Is it really crooked?"

"A little bit," said Melissa cautiously. She couldn't believe Alice had done it.

"Now for the other side." In a few seconds, Alice had sliced off the end of her other braid. She gave her head a shake. "It feels good. Freer. I like it."

Until you look in a mirror, thought Melissa. Alice's hair looked like it had been attacked by Cody with a pair of his play scissors.

"I'm glad I did it." Alice laid the two ends of the braids on the shelf. Melissa's stomach felt queasy when she looked at them. Alice waved the knife at Melissa. "Want a trim?"

Melissa's hands flew to her ponytail. "No!"

"I'm just kidding. Let's go swimming. I want to see what my hair feels like when it gets wet."

"You didn't stay very long," protested Alice when Melissa, drowsy from baking on the flat rock, climbed into her canoe. Alice's hair had dried into a fluffy cloud that made her narrow face look softer.

"I'll come earlier tomorrow," promised Melissa.

"You could bring your little brother," said Alice. "I wouldn't mind."

Bring Cody to Dar Wynd? That would wreck everything.

"Forget it," said Melissa. She gave a few strong strokes with her paddle and then turned to call goodbye. But Alice had vanished into the trees.

Melissa stretched her legs in front of her as she paddled. She was starting to get a tan. She thought vaguely of checking at the store to see if they had any nail polish so she could paint her toenails. Alice's toenails were painted black, but she could imagine what Sharlene would say if she painted hers black too. Purple, maybe. She could ask Alice what she thought.

Melissa realized that she didn't care anymore that Alice had lied about the tree house. It might even be partly true. She and Austin had probably fixed it up.

Alice was the best friend that Melissa had ever had. She made all the kids at school seem boring. You never knew what she was going to say or do next. And she hadn't mentioned the pact to jump off the cliff today. Maybe, just maybe, she had forgotten all about it.

Thirteen

The next day, Alice was waiting for Melissa on the flat rock. "We're not going to make the arrows anymore," she said as Melissa tied her canoe to the overhanging branch. "It was kind of dumb anyway. I've got something way better." Her thin face was tight with excitement.

"What is it?"

"It's a surprise. It's at Dar Wynd."

Melissa followed Alice along the path through the trees. Her feet were bare today and the ground felt hot and parched. The leaves on the bushes had a gray dusty look. A patch of wild purple daisies at the edge of the clearing had withered in the heat.

A long thin object wrapped in a white towel lay on the floor in the middle of the tree house. Melissa stared in amazement as Alice folded back the towel and uncovered a gleaming silver sword with a long narrow blade attached to an ornate handle.

Melissa gasped. "Is it real?"

"Of course it's real." For a second, Alice looked annoyed. "Austin gave it to me. Well, *lent* it really. But he said I can keep it all summer."

"Where did he get it?" breathed Melissa.

"He has a whole collection of swords. He orders them off the Internet. This is his best one. He wanted me to take it."

"It's amazing," said Melissa.

"Pick it up. Hold it," said Alice.

Melissa carefully picked up the sword. It was very heavy. The blade shimmered and was almost as long as her arm. The handle, fashioned from a darker metal, was a monster's head with sharp curved horns and long claws that gripped the top of the blade.

Melissa swung the sword back and forth gently. "What does he do with it?" she said.

"Nothing," said Alice. She sounded impatient. "He has all his swords on his wall. He collects them. Elfrida's going to have a sword just like this. Her brother Warwick gives it to her. She can use it to battle the fairies."

Melissa put the sword back on the floor. It made her feel a little sick.

"I'm going to write about the sword now," said Alice. "While I'm feeling inspired. You can read one of my books if you want."

Alice's books with the monsters and weird fantasy creatures on the covers didn't interest Melissa at all. "Do you have any blank paper here?" she asked.

Alice opened her red binder and took out a sheet of paper. Melissa found a pencil on the shelf. She leaned her back against the wall and used the binder for a table. Alice sat cross-legged, flipping through a pile of papers covered with writing.

Melissa slid into her drawing. She was hesitant at first and then drew quickly, shutting out everything else around her. She was startled when she heard Alice crumple up a piece of paper and say crossly, "I can't do it today. I can't write."

Alice stood up and peered over Melissa's shoulder. Melissa resisted the urge to cover her drawing with her hand. Her back tensed.

"Hey, that's good," said Alice. She sounded shocked. "Really, really good. I didn't know you could draw like that."

Melissa shrugged. She didn't say anything but she glowed inside. She had drawn a girl dressed in a tunic and tall boots. Her hair was tucked under a cap, but you could tell she was a girl because of her delicate features. She was holding a sword that looked exactly like the sword Austin had given Alice.

"It's Elfrida, isn't it?" said Alice.

Melissa nodded. "People are hard to draw," she said.

"I think she looks like me," said Alice.

"I used your face," said Melissa.

Alice studied the drawing for a moment. "Can I keep it?"

"If you want." Melissa handed her the paper and the binder. "It's not that great."

"But I love it!" Alice seemed unable to pull her eyes away from the drawing. Finally she put it carefully in the back of the binder, snapped the rings shut and put the binder on the floor beside her scattered papers.

Melissa stood up and stretched. She could feel a rim of sweat on her upper lip. "It's so hot today. Do you want to go swimming?"

"Not at the rock. That's getting boring." Alice's pleasure over the drawing seemed to have evaporated and a small frown darkened her pale face. She picked up a mug and then set it down restlessly. "I'm going to change the rules," she said suddenly.

"What rules?" A tickle of apprehension ran up Melissa's spine.

"I'm going to jump today." Alice stared at Melissa and burst into laughter. "You should see your face!

116

I didn't say *you* had to jump. You still have another five days. But I'm going to do it!"

Melissa's stomach turned to water. "Why now?" she said weakly.

"Because," said Alice, "I can't write and there's nothing else to do." Her eyes glowed. "You have to come with me. I need a witness."

The little cove was in dappled shade, the water smooth and deep green. Even out of the direct sun it was broiling hot. Melissa had worked up a sweat paddling and she leaned over the edge of the canoe and splashed water on her face. A small brown bird hopped through an overhanging bush, and Melissa imagined she could hear the dusty leaves crackle with the heat.

The cliff was even higher than she remembered. It loomed above them, the rocks at the top shimmering white in the sunlight. Alice had chatted all the way over but was silent now. They tied the canoe to the dead tree and climbed up the trail. The air was thick with the smell of pine needles, and the heat felt like a heavy blanket on Melissa's shoulders.

When they got to the top, Alice walked right across the rocks to the edge and peered over. "It doesn't look that bad," she announced.

Melissa hung back. If she went any closer she would feel dizzy. "Are you sure it's safe? You don't want to hit a rock or something."

"In that deep water? And I told you Austin did it." Alice sounded impatient. She stripped off her shorts and top and stood poised in her red bathing suit. "Count to five for me. Then I'll go."

Melissa licked her dry lips. "One…two…three… four…five."

At the last minute she thought Alice was going to back out. Alice hesitated and her back went rigid. Then she took a deep breath, spread her arms apart like wings and jumped.

Melissa heard a huge splash.

She waited a few seconds and then called, "Alice?"

From the middle of the lake a loon gave a long warbling cry. A bumblebee droning in a patch of tall white clover was the only other sound breaking the silence.

Melissa had expected Alice to shout out something, tell her how great it was, urge her to not be such a baby, to jump too. "Alice?" she called again.

She edged closer to the edge of the cliff. She shouldn't be such a scaredy-cat. It wasn't as if the cliff was suddenly going to collapse. But she could feel her heart pounding in her chest.

She got close enough so she could see down into the bay to the spot where she figured Alice must have landed. A widening circle of ripples spread across the smooth water. There was no sign of Alice.

"Alice!" A wave of panic rose in Melissa's throat. There was no way Alice could hold her breath all that time. She imagined all kinds of terrible things—Alice somehow caught in the weeds or knocked unconscious from hitting a submerged log.

Help, I need to get help, thought Melissa frantically. She backed away from the cliff and plunged down the trail, her feet skidding on the brown pine needles. She frantically recited instructions over and over in her head—untie the canoe, paddle back to the cabin, get Sharlene.

Melissa fumbled with the rope. She looked up and scanned the bay one last time.

"Hey, wait for me!" said Alice's voice.

She was treading water, right up against the bottom of the cliff, deep in shadow. She swam toward the canoe with strong strokes. Melissa's legs felt weak with relief. She took big breaths to steady her slowly growing anger.

"That wasn't funny," said Melissa when Alice stood up in the shallow water beside the canoe.

Alice made her eyes huge. "What?"

"I thought you had drowned." Melissa knew she sounded pathetic, but she couldn't help it. "Why did you hide like that?"

Alice looked like she was about to protest, but then she shrugged her thin shoulders and said, "It was just a joke. You don't have to get so mad."

"Well, it wasn't a joke to me," said Melissa furiously.

She waited stiffly in the canoe while Alice climbed back up to the top for her clothes. They paddled to the island in silence. I'm going back to the cabin, thought Melissa. As soon as we get to the island, I'm going to the cabin.

But as they were nearing the flat rock, her anger slowly melted away and curiosity overcame her. "So what was it like, anyway?" she said grudgingly.

Alice's words came out in a gush. "Great! Awesome! I felt like an eagle. You wait until it's your turn, Melissa. You just wait!"

Fourteen

When Sharlene announced the next day that she was going to the store for an ice run, Melissa said, "I'm coming too."

She didn't really like staying at the cabin by herself. She was afraid that the man with the dragon tattoo and his friend might come back. Sharlene had said confidently that they wouldn't, that they had got the message, but Melissa didn't know how her mother could be absolutely sure.

When they got to the store, Marge was full of talk about a forest fire burning in the valley next to them. "They've got forty firefighters and three helicopters over there. They're dive-bombing it with water. It's why the sky is so hazy today. That's not cloud, it's smoke."

"You can smell it," said Melissa. She was peeling the paper off an ice-cream bar for Cody. She wondered how long it took forest fires to travel. How far away exactly was this valley?

But Marge seemed more excited than worried. "Started with a cigarette," she said. "Can you believe it?"

Sharlene bought the ice, a blueberry pie, an air mattress and three lime green noodles to play with in the lake. On the way back to the cabin she talked about planning something for Melissa's twelfth birthday. It was coming up quickly, just two days away.

Melissa never let herself get her hopes up about her birthday. She snorted when Sharlene said casually that they should think about a little party. "You and me and Cody? That sounds like fun."

In the old days that would have bugged Sharlene. She would have attacked Melissa for her poor attitude and they would have ended up yelling at each other. Melissa realized suddenly that it was a long time since she had heard Sharlene lose her temper.

"You could ask Alice," Sharlene said calmly. "And I think Bonnie would come. She told me she loves getting breaks from the guest ranch."

The last time Bonnie had visited, Sharlene had accused Melissa of being rude. But she seemed to have forgotten about that. Maybe it isn't such a bad idea, thought Melissa. Most of her birthdays had passed by almost unnoticed. She had never had a real party like the other kids at school.

"Where would we get a cake?" she said.

"We'll be creative," said Sharlene. "We'll think of something. There might even be something at the store. We'll invite Alice and Bonnie for lunch."

"I guess so," said Melissa.

She tried to imagine Alice with her family. Would she like Sharlene? And what would she think of Cody? Melissa sighed. She hoped she wouldn't regret this.

A dark blue pickup truck with printing and a round crest on the side and a boat strapped onto a roof rack was parked beside the cabin when they got back. A man was standing at the side door. Melissa read the side of the truck. *Conservation Officer*. She looked at the man curiously. He was wearing a blue shirt and gray pants and had a wide belt weighted down with pouches. A black gun gleamed in a holster.

"Hi there," he called out. "Just checking in on you. Heard you were staying out here. How are things going?"

"Fine," said Sharlene. "Just let me get this ice in the cooler before it melts in my arms."

"That will take all of about five seconds in

this heat," said the man cheerfully. He introduced himself as Ted Stoneridge and stood back while Melissa opened the door with one hand, a grocery bag propped in her other arm.

Ted ended up staying for iced tea. He and Sharlene sat side by side in lawn chairs on the porch, Cody curled in Sharlene's lap, and chatted easily with each other. Melissa sat on the steps, sipping tea and listening.

Ted had more information on the fire. It had flared up in the night and the area burning had increased to thirty square kilometers.

"Are we in danger here?" said Sharlene.

"Not at the moment," said Ted. "I'll keep checking in on you folks though. I'll be around the area a lot. You'd be surprised how many people think they should still be allowed to have campfires. They have no idea how quickly a fire can get out of control."

Melissa glanced at the puckered scar on her hand. This was the cue for Sharlene to say, "We had a bad experience with a fire once," and then go into all the details that were nobody's business, especially not Ted's. She tensed, but Sharlene just played with Cody's hair.

"If the fire heads this way, there's a remote chance you'll have to be evacuated," said Ted.

"We could be out in a few minutes," Sharlene said. "We don't have much stuff. I'd hate to get trapped down here."

"I won't let that happen to you," said Ted warmly. He drained his glass of iced tea and folded his large brown hands in his lap. He seemed reluctant to leave. He *likes* Sharlene, Melissa suddenly realized.

Melissa did a quick assessment. He was sort of good-looking in an outdoorsy way. She wondered idly if he were married. She peered at his hand to see if he was wearing a wedding ring but it was impossible to tell. It had been two years since Darren left. Her mother hadn't even gone on a single date since then. She didn't seem interested anymore. And Melissa couldn't imagine her mother going out with someone like Ted, who called people *folks*. Ted seemed nice enough, but Melissa was glad when he finally left and it was just the three of them again.

Alice looked pleased when Melissa invited her to her birthday.

"Don't bring a present," Melissa said awkwardly. "It's not that kind of party." She felt a pang of worry. Did Alice go to birthday parties all the time, the kind the kids at school talked about? "It's not even a real party," she added quickly. "We're just going to have lunch."

The girls were sitting cross-legged on the floor of the tree house. Alice had brought a jar of lemonade and a plastic container holding four cupcakes with pink icing and tiny purple and yellow sprinkles shaped like flowers. While she ate, Melissa couldn't pull her eyes away from the sword, gleaming against the wall. She had never known that ordinary people owned things like that. She licked icing from her finger. "These are delicious," she said.

"Mom and I baked them last night," said Alice.

Melissa had brought her sketchbook, and when they were finished eating she worked on a drawing of the tree house while Alice wrote. After a while Alice handed Melissa a sheet of paper. "Read this and tell me what you think."

Melissa closed her sketchbook, leaned back against the wall of the tree house and began to read.

Warwick pulled the sword from its sheath. It gleamed in the firelight flickering in the great stone fireplace. Elfrida's back prickled with goose bumps.

"This was Papa's sword," said Warwick. "He gave it to me on the battlefield at Great Tor when he fell. With his last breath he said, 'This sword has killed many enemies and has served me well. It is time for it to serve you now.'"

Warwick handed the sword to Elfrida. She gasped when her hand touched the cold metal.

"Curse my leg!" spat out Warwick. "It should be me going on this dangerous mission. And curse the spriggans who have stolen our brother!" His dark eyes gleamed and he touched his sister's cheek softly. "Go with speed and be careful," he said hoarsely. A sob escaped from him. "Please, God, do not take my sister away from me too!"

Elfrida's eyes filled with tears.

"There is no time to lose," whispered Warwick. "The sword will keep you safe. Go now and bring our little brother back."

"It's great," said Melissa, putting down the paper. "I like Warwick."

"He's actually a lot like Austin," said Alice. "Warwick and Elfrida are very close. Warwick would do anything for his family. He's so angry that he can't rescue Tristan himself."

Alice was talking about them as if they were real people again. She had an amazing imagination. Melissa knew she could never have made up such a story. "What happens next?" she asked.

"Elfrida and the old woman, Mareea, travel to the pass above the valley where the spriggans have taken Tristan." Alice frowned. "They're traveling on the horses and they can take some stuff but not a lot. So they'll have to hunt and gather berries and dig up roots and stuff like that on the way. I've been looking around on this island to see if there's anything I could try so I can get the feeling. But I haven't found much."

"They could make bannock," suggested Melissa. "It's kind of like a wilderness bread."

She wasn't sure that Alice wanted her ideas but Alice stared at her and said, "What do you mean?"

"We made some two days ago," said Melissa. "We fried it in a frying pan but Mom said you can wrap it around a stick and cook it in a fire."

"Exactly how do you make it?" said Alice.

"It's just flour and water and baking powder and something called lard," said Melissa. "We used margarine."

"I know what lard is," said Alice. "It's like fat. Elfrida could use…" She hesitated for a second. "Bacon grease."

Melissa suddenly thought of something. "They probably didn't have baking powder in those days."

"I'll leave it out," said Alice promptly. She sounded excited. "It won't make that much difference. But I need to know how much flour and stuff."

The recipe was easy to remember. While Melissa recited the amounts, Alice wrote quickly on a piece of paper. "It's a really good idea," she said. "I'm going to put it in my story."

Melissa felt her cheeks flush with pleasure. "Thanks," she mumbled.

Alice jumped up. "Come on. I want to do some more exploring. I haven't looked everywhere yet. There must be some berries or *something* to eat somewhere on this island!"

The girls followed a path through some low willow bushes, which Alice said might have been made by deer. It ended at a low grassy bank at the edge of the water. Melissa could see far down the lake from this end of the island, but she couldn't see the Hopes' ranch.

"Our house is right behind that point of land sticking out," said Alice. "It's at the very end of the lake."

Melissa's face felt hot. It would sound weird if she told Alice now that she knew that, that she had paddled past the ranch and even seen Austin. It would seem like she had been trying to hide something. So she just said, "Oh."

She and Alice tried pulling up a few plants to see what the roots looked like, but the ground was hard and dry and they made no headway, even with a sharp stick. They explored a few more trails that petered out quickly. While they wandered, Alice talked about her jump off the cliff—how fantastic it had been and how it wasn't really scary at all. Melissa's stomach tightened in a knot. She had four more days until she had to tell Alice that she wasn't going to do it. She didn't want to think about it.

"They always say in books that they survived on roots and berries," grumbled Alice finally, "but a person would starve around here."

Alice seemed to have lost interest and said she had to get home. The girls left the island together, gliding in their canoes side by side for a few minutes until Alice said goodbye and headed down the lake.

Melissa, hot and scratched and itchy from some mosquito bites, paddled lazily toward their dock, thinking first about her birthday and then about the more immediate plan of spending the rest of the day floating on the air mattress.

Fifteen

The next morning Cody screamed and kicked when Melissa tried to plunk him on the air mattress. His body was wet and slippery and he thrashed about like a fish.

It was no use spending any more time making him put his face in the water. He refused. Melissa climbed on the mattress and lay on her stomach, one eye on Cody, who had forgotten his anger and splashed happily in the shallow water with the noodles.

At lunch Sharlene announced that she had finished her first essay and that it was "pretty good, considering I'm so out of practice."

"Why *did* you quit high school?" blurted Melissa.

Sharlene sighed. "The only group I fit in with was the party group. None of us were interested in learning anything. I look back now and think *what a waste*."

Melissa finished her tuna sandwich in silence. One more year and she would be leaving elementary school. She was pretty sure she wasn't going to fit in with any group at her new school. The party group at least sounded popular.

As if Sharlene read her mind, she said, "Hanging out with the party kids wasn't as much fun as it sounds. It was pretty boring most of the time." She reached out and touched Melissa's shoulder. Without meaning to, Melissa drew back and Sharlene dropped her hand. "I wasted a lot of my life, Mel," she said. "You're much smarter than me, thank goodness."

Uncomfortable, Melissa changed the subject. "Are we still having my birthday party tomorrow?"

Sharlene looked surprised. "Of course we are. Cody and I have some things to do today to get ready, don't we, Cody? It's going to be fun. And I can't wait to meet Alice."

As she paddled to the island, Melissa tried to imagine Alice with Sharlene and Cody. Alice's family sounded so normal. Her mother was an important person and very busy, but she always seemed to have time to do stuff with Alice. She even had time to bake fancy cupcakes. And having an older brother like Austin was a hundred times better than having a pesky little brother who was as much work as Cody.

When Melissa got to the flat rock, Alice's blue canoe wasn't there. Surprised, Melissa drifted. A dragonfly with shimmering wings rested on her paddle. There was not a breath of wind, and the island had an oddly deserted feeling.

Where *was* Alice?

Maybe Austin had finally finished haying and he and Alice were hanging out together. Melissa felt a pang of jealousy, and for a horrible moment she wondered if Dar Wynd was over. Then she shrugged away her thoughts irritably. She was overreacting. She decided to go to the tree house and get her sketchbook, which she had forgotten the day before. If Alice didn't come by then, she would go back to the cabin.

It took Melissa a moment to find the sketchbook. Alice had been back, either the previous night or in the morning. She had tidied things up, and the sketchbook was on the end of the board shelf. The sleeping bag was rolled up and Alice's writing things were neatly stacked beside the sketchbook. There were a few new things on the shelf: another fantasy book with a bookmark in it, a glass jar containing drooping yellow wildflowers, and a slim brown leather book with the edge of a photograph poking out of the back. It didn't look like Alice had given up Dar Wynd after all.

Curious, Melissa opened the leather book. The pages inside were blank except for the first page, where Alice had written the words *Dar Wynd, August 7*, and then one short sentence. *Mother had a good day today.* Melissa frowned. August 7 was yesterday, so Alice must have written that last night. What did that mean? Then she remembered that Alice had said something about a special dinner celebrating a book contract or something.

The book was like a journal. Melissa had never seen the point in keeping a journal. She had tried once, but why write down all the boring things that you were doing? She slid the photograph out of the back and studied it.

It was a picture of Alice standing between two boys in front of a small white house. They were smiling—big happy grins that lit up their faces—and Melissa imagined the person taking the photograph making a funny face or saying something to make them laugh. She immediately recognized Austin, the tall boy with the dark hair that hung over his face. He had his arm around Alice. The other boy was little, about Cody's age, with skinny arms and legs. Alice and Austin were wearing jeans and T-shirts, but the little boy was in a bathing suit and his tummy bulged out like a balloon.

Cody's tummy did that too, when he had just eaten. Melissa wondered who the little boy was. A cousin, maybe, who had been visiting. She looked at the photograph for a moment longer and then slid it back into the journal and replaced it on the shelf.

Melissa picked up her sketchbook and climbed down the ladder. Dar Wynd was a different place without Alice—too quiet and very lonely.

"You're back early," said Sharlene. She firmly closed the door to the bedroom that she and Cody shared, but not before Melissa had a glimpse of presents wrapped in bright paper on the bottom bunk bed and a pile of blown-up purple balloons on the floor.

"Remember, Cody, big boys keep secrets," said Sharlene.

"Alice wasn't there," said Melissa. She wondered what she should do for the rest of the day and then decided to finish her drawing of the tree house.

Melissa interspersed drawing with dips in the lake and a supper break when she offered to make grilled cheese sandwiches for everyone so Sharlene could work on her English course. She finished the drawing just before it was time for bed. She had bought thumb-tacks at the store and had covered almost an entire wall in her little bedroom with her pictures. She tacked up the drawing of the tree house and then lay on her bed and studied it.

It was one of her best. She had worked hard to get the texture of the bark on the big tree and the weath-ered boards just right. She thought about the art camp in Kelowna that she had wanted to go to so badly. It seemed a long time ago now that she had brought home the brochure. She rolled over onto her side. The loons called back and forth on the lake, making the back of Melissa's neck prickle with goose bumps, and she wondered if that was a little bit what a wolf sounded like. Her last thought before sleep was that if she had gone to art camp, she would never have heard a loon. She would never have paddled a canoe. She would never have met Alice.

Sixteen

On Melissa's birthday morning the haze and the smoky smell had disappeared and the sky was deep blue again. Sharlene, Melissa and Cody went to the store. Sharlene made Melissa stay in the truck and came out carrying something in a green garbage bag.

"Marge says the fire is still burning," she reported. "It's grown by another ten square kilometers. But the wind has changed. That's why the air has cleared."

Sharlene settled the garbage bag on Cody's lap. "Don't tip it," she warned. Melissa pretended not to know what it was but she had a pretty good idea there was a box with a birthday cake inside. A woman in the area baked goodies for Marge to sell at the store. Sharlene and Marge had had a long whispered conversation the last time they were at the store, and Melissa had distinctly heard the word *cake*.

Bonnie arrived first with a small package wrapped in pale yellow tissue paper. "I know you said no presents, but this is something small," she said. She gave Melissa a hug, which made her stiffen because they didn't really even know each other. Then she hugged Sharlene and Cody, so Melissa supposed she was just a hugging kind of person.

"Thank you," Melissa said awkwardly, putting Bonnie's gift on the table with four other packages that Cody had been hovering around all morning. She worried that Alice would see the presents and feel badly. "Maybe I should open these now," she said.

"Oh, let's wait for Alice," said Sharlene. "Part of the fun of a birthday party is watching people open their presents."

"Here she comes!" yelled Cody. He had been watching the lake like a hawk, not quite clear exactly who Alice was and where she was coming from. "She's Melissa's friend," Sharlene had explained patiently over and over. "She lives in that house we saw at the end of the lake. Melissa plays with her every afternoon on the island."

To Melissa's relief, Sharlene let her go down to the dock by herself to greet Alice. "You stay with me, Cody," Sharlene said, grabbing the excited little boy by his arm. "You can bring the presents outside."

Alice tied up her canoe, and the girls walked up the grassy bank to the cabin. Sharlene had attached the purple balloons to the posts that held up the porch roof. In the middle of the porch she had arranged an assortment of lawn chairs, two of the chairs that belonged with the kitchen table, and a small round table that she had found in the shed. She had spread a green cloth over the table and had produced bright party napkins and paper plates from somewhere. Melissa worried that Alice would think it was dumb, but Alice said enthusiastically, "Wow! Everything looks so nice!"

Melissa had a sudden horrifying picture of Bonnie and Sharlene both trying to hug Alice at the same time, but Bonnie just said, "Hi there," and Sharlene smiled and said, "It's great to meet you, Alice."

"I'm Cody," said Cody loudly. His arms were full of presents which he dumped in the middle of the table.

For a second, Alice just stared at the little boy. The bit of color drained out of her face, and Melissa wondered if something was wrong. Then Alice squatted down in front of him. "Hi Cody," she said in a serious voice. "How are you doing?"

"Good," he mumbled, instantly shy. He stuck his thumb in his mouth and retreated closer to Melissa.

Alice had brought an envelope, which she put beside the presents. Sharlene said, "Everyone sit.

Cody, you can help me bring out some cold drinks."

"I want to sit beside Alice," shouted Cody, his shyness forgotten.

"I'll save you a seat," said Alice, and Melissa felt a flush of gratitude. Alice was being nice to Cody. Maybe they could get through this party without one of his tantrums.

That's how she had been thinking of the party—as something to get through safely without being embarrassed—but it was turning out to be fun. Bonnie and Sharlene filled up any quiet spaces with chatter, and Alice seemed relaxed.

"Melissa tells me your mother works for a publishing company," said Sharlene at one point. "That must be interesting work."

"Oh, it is," said Alice. "She's very good at it. She's really busy right now but she's been meaning to ask you over. She's going to invite you for a barbecue as soon as her contract is finished."

Melissa saw a slight look of surprise flicker across Bonnie's face. There was a tiny pause and then Sharlene said smoothly, "That would be lovely."

During their lunch of ham sandwiches, veggies and dip and potato chips, Melissa opened her presents. Bonnie had given her a shiny new horseshoe with a gold ribbon tied to it. "Hang it over your bedroom door," she said. "It will give you luck." She explained how it was important to put the open end at the top so the luck didn't run out, and Melissa thanked her.

She opened Sharlene's and Cody's gifts next. There was a brand-new sketchbook and a box of charcoals, a book called *Nail Art* that had six little bottles of fluorescent nail polish with it, a silver heart pendant on a delicate chain that Melissa fell in love with instantly and a blow-up beach toy.

Cody hopped around as she pulled the plastic wrap off the toy. "It's a seal," said Sharlene. "Marge just got them in. I think Cody's hoping he can play with it too."

Melissa thought she was too old for a blow-up seal and knew that Cody's pestering was probably why Sharlene had bought it. She picked up Alice's envelope.

She could feel Alice watching her carefully while she tore it open. She took out a homemade card with the words *Happy Birthday Melissa* written in felt pen across the front. Melissa opened it. Inside were two crisp twenty-dollar bills.

Sharlene saw them at the same time Melissa did and said, "Oh, Alice, that wasn't at all necessary. That's far too much."

"It's not every day your best friend has a birthday," said Alice.

Best friend. The words stunned Melissa. She felt her cheeks burn. Sharlene looked surprised too, but she recovered quickly and said, "Well, it's terribly generous of you. I'm sure Melissa will buy something special with it."

Melissa realized that she hadn't said anything and mumbled, "Thank you."

At that moment Ted arrived, in a different vehicle this time, a green Jeep. Instead of his uniform he was dressed in ordinary jeans, running shoes and a short-sleeved plaid shirt. "You're just in time for birthday cake," called Sharlene as Melissa tucked the money carefully back into the envelope.

Melissa hadn't seen the cake, which had been hidden in a cupboard, until Sharlene carried it out, ablaze with twelve candles. A jolt ran through her. The tall round cake was covered with pink icing dotted with sprinkles like tiny flowers.

Exactly the same as the cupcakes Alice had said her mother had baked. Melissa couldn't look at Alice. Her head whirled. Alice had obviously lied again. It was just too big a coincidence. The cupcakes must have come from the store. But why would Alice lie about a thing like that? What was the point?

Alice didn't seem embarrassed. She didn't even seem to have noticed. Melissa shrugged away her confusion. She wasn't going to let a small thing like that wreck her birthday. She blew out the candles and everyone clapped and cheered.

"One more year and you'll have a teenager living in your house, Shar," teased Bonnie. "Fun and games. Just you wait. I know. I've raised three."

After they finished the cake, everyone helped blow up the seal, and Melissa, Cody and Alice took it down to the water.

Melissa discovered happily that twelve *wasn't* too old for a huge blow-up black seal, which Cody named Sammy. Alice and Melissa took turns trying to sit on its slippery back, laughing when it popped out from underneath them or they tumbled off sideways into the water.

"Me too! Me too!" screeched Cody. Alice lifted him up and he straddled the seal, his legs clamped tightly and his hands clutching Alice's waist.

Melissa grew bored with the seal after a while and collapsed on the air mattress. Alice seemed to have endless patience. She pushed Cody, who was perched on the seal, back and forth through the shallow water. "Keep going!" he shouted.

"You're going to have a friend for life!" Sharlene called out. "You'll have to come back every day or we'll have no peace."

Later, when Melissa, Alice and Cody were sitting on their towels on the grass, slurping watermelon, Sharlene said, "You're wonderful with little kids, Alice.

You must have some younger cousins or something. Or else do a lot of babysitting."

Melissa thought instantly of the photograph with the little blond boy who reminded her of Cody. But Alice just said, "I like little kids, that's all."

Bonnie and Ted left. Cody fell asleep in a lawn chair and Sharlene scooped him up and carried him to his bunk bed. Alice hung around for the afternoon and looked shocked when Sharlene said it was five o'clock.

"She seemed upset, didn't she?" mused Sharlene when Alice had hurried off. "Do you think there was something wrong?"

"I don't know," said Melissa, frowning. She and Alice almost always left the island together, and it was usually around four o'clock. They had never stayed as late as five.

"Like Cinderella hurrying home from the ball," said Sharlene thoughtfully.

In the evening, Melissa brought the *Nail Art* book outside, and she and Sharlene sat on lawn chairs and painted their fingernails. There were pages of ideas for designs: flowers, ducks, grapes, hearts, clouds and even a tea pot. It was hard to decide. In the end

Melissa opted for a different-colored butterfly on each fingernail. Sharlene said she couldn't compete with an artist like Melissa and settled for purple and blue stripes.

"I like Alice a lot," said Sharlene, sticking one hand out to admire the effect. "She was awfully good with Cody. He's already asking when she's coming back."

Melissa didn't say anything. She concentrated on her blue butterfly's wings.

"Bonnie says there's some kind of mystery surrounding the family. Alice's older brother has done some jobs for them at the guest ranch and she said you can't get two words in a row out of him. And she's never seen the mother even though the family's been living here almost two years. That's a little odd."

"Alice's mom is away a lot. She has an important job. And anyway, everyone isn't like you," said Melissa. "Friends with the whole community. And besides, Alice says they're going to ask us over for a barbecue soon."

"Mmmm," said Sharlene. She screwed the lid on the bottle of purple nail polish and said, "Done."

Melissa flipped pages in the book, careful not to smudge her butterflies. "Do you think Cody's toenails are big enough for this?" she asked, showing Sharlene a green snake with its head on a big toe and its long body crawling across the other toenails.

"Yup, just barely," said Sharlene. "He'll love it."

Seventeen

Alice was waiting for Melissa at Dar Wynd the next day. She had been writing, but she put down her pen and jumped up when Melissa appeared. "Look what I've got," she said. She picked up a round foil-covered package from the shelf. "Guess."

"I don't know," said Melissa.

"I'll give you a hint. It's something to do with food. And it was your idea."

Melissa stared at her blankly and Alice said triumphantly, "It's bannock dough. I made it last night."

She unwrapped the foil. Inside was a mound of soft white dough. Her hazel eyes flashed. "We're going to cook it," she said. "We'll do it like you said, wrapped around a stick."

It took a few seconds for Melissa to digest what Alice meant. "You mean on a fire?"

"How else?" said Alice. Her words were sharp but she was smiling.

Melissa's heart gave a jump. "Wait a minute," she said. "You can't light a fire."

"I know how," said Alice, and Melissa thought she was deliberately pretending not to understand. "And I've got matches and paper."

"But you can't. There's a ban on all campfires. Haven't you heard about the forest fire?" Melissa felt panic rise inside her. Alice looked like she was serious.

"That's miles away," said Alice airily. "Who cares? We're not going to light a big fire. Just big enough to cook the bannock."

"You're crazy," said Melissa. "You could burn the whole island down."

"Nothing's going to happen."

Melissa searched frantically for arguments. "It's windy. You can't light a fire in this wind."

There was a pause. Then Alice said coldly, "It's so hard to do stuff with you, Melissa."

"That's not true," said Melissa, stung.

Alice sighed heavily. "Well, I'm going to do it. I don't care if you help or not."

Alice had left a bucket with a few pieces of

newspaper and a box of matches in it at the bottom of the ladder. She retrieved the bucket, surveyed the clearing for a moment and then walked over to a place in the middle. "We'll build it away from the trees," she said. "I'm not entirely stupid."

"You're going to build it *here*?" said Melissa. "So far away from the water?"

Alice frowned. Then she said, "You're right. It would be better beside the lake. Come on. I'll bring this stuff and you bring the bannock."

Melissa followed Alice along the trail. When they got to the canoes she would tell Alice she was leaving. "I *did* think of water, in case you're wondering," said Alice over her shoulder. "That's what I brought the bucket for."

"You could build it right in the middle of the rock," said Melissa when they got to the flat rock. "That would be safest."

"Stop worrying," said Alice. "I don't want to mess up the rock for sunbathing. We'll put it here." She kicked a patch of ground on the bank.

I should leave now, thought Melissa. But she didn't. She watched Alice pull up clumps of dry grass until she had a small circle of bare dirt. Then Alice started to tear the newspaper into strips, making a pile.

"You need rocks," said Melissa.

Sharlene had told Melissa how she and her sister

Eleanor had roasted hot dogs and marshmallows over outdoor fires. She had described how they had collected large rocks to make a protective circle and said they would do that if the fire ban ever lifted. Alice didn't seem to have any idea how to do this properly, and Melissa knew at that moment that she was going to stay. "You need to make a circle of rocks," she said. "To keep the fire out of the grass."

Alice hesitated, then said, "Okay, if it makes you happy."

The rocks proved hard to find, but after about ten minutes of searching they had a small pile. "I think they should really be bigger," said Melissa, unhappily, as they arranged them in a circle.

"It's good enough," said Alice impatiently. "How many times do I have to tell you? We're just building a little fire."

Melissa filled the bucket with water and set it beside the circle of rocks. Alice gathered up dry sticks from the ground. She made a small teepee of sticks over the shredded newspaper.

The newspaper caught instantly with only one match, and in a few seconds the sticks crackled and snapped.

Alice stood up. "We're going to need bigger sticks," she said. "Those little ones are burning up too fast."

Alice hunted for wood in the trees while Melissa

guarded the tiny flames. By the time Alice was back, the fire was out.

"Why didn't you keep it going?" demanded Alice as she dumped an armful of thick branches on the ground.

"It was burning too fast," said Melissa.

Alice frowned. "We'll need a stick that doesn't burn to wrap the bannock on. You can get that while I get some more small stuff to get this started again."

Melissa gazed around uncertainly. There were a couple of big evergreen trees near the edge of the lake with bare branches sticking out of their trunks, but when she broke one off it was so dry it made a loud crack like a gunshot. She decided on the clump of bushy green willows where her canoe was tied. She slipped off her runners, waded out into the water and tried to break off a sturdy branch. It bent but didn't break and she had to twist it back and forth before it came free. It was a bit floppy, but Melissa couldn't think of anything else.

She scrambled back up on the bank. The fire was burning brightly again. "Don't you think that's enough wood?" she said as Alice fed more sticks into the blaze. The wind had picked up a little and the flames were being blown sideways.

"One more piece," said Alice. "Then we'll let it die down and cook the bannock."

She picked up a thick heavy branch covered with dry gray moss and laid it over the top of the fire. It caught instantly, shooting flames high above it. A blast of heat seared Melissa's cheeks.

"What are you doing?" she gasped. Even Alice looked frightened as the flames shot higher and higher, veering wildly to the side in the wind.

Melissa had a horrifying vision of the flames streaking up the trunks of the nearby trees into the leafy canopy above. She tried to grab the end of the branch that hadn't caught on fire yet and drag it off. But the heat was too intense and in a few seconds it was too late; the entire branch was engulfed in flame.

Melissa remembered Ted talking about the forest fire at her party the day before. *It jumped the river*, he had said. *In two places*. Melissa didn't know how a fire crossed water. When Ted was talking, she had imagined a fiery ball flying through the air.

How wide was the river? If fire could jump across a river, it could jump from this island to the mainland.

Melissa picked up the bucket and hurled the water on top of the soaring flames. There was a huge sizzling sound and a mass of steam.

"Hey, what are you doing? Quit that!" shouted Alice, but Melissa ignored her. She filled the bucket again and dumped it on the smoldering fire.

More steam. The rocks hissed and spat. Melissa didn't stop until she had dumped four buckets of water on the pile of blackened charred sticks. She took a big breath to calm her racing heart. Alice's face was white with fury. "You shouldn't have done that."

"It was way too big," said Melissa, trembling. "It was going to catch those trees on fire." She bent down and stirred the sodden mass of black wood with a stick, reassuring herself that it was out.

"I had it under control." Alice's words were icy. "You freaked because of your stupid kitchen catching on fire."

Not kitchen, thought Melissa, suddenly feeling like she was going to throw up. Trailer. The whole trailer. "That had nothing to do with it," she said, fighting back tears that pooled behind her eyelids. She stood up slowly on weak legs.

"Yeah, right. Well, you wrecked this. There's no point trying again." Alice kicked fiercely at one of the blackened rocks. "I'm going back to Dar Wynd," she said, sounding disgusted. "You can do what you want."

"I'm going home," said Melissa.

Melissa woke up suddenly, her heart racing. Her back was soaked with sweat. The fire dream was always the same. Flames sweeping up the curtains, Darren shouting, smoke everywhere.

Melissa lay still for a minute, waiting for the images to fade. She sometimes wondered if that was how it had really happened. There had been plastic blinds in the kitchen, and when they had gone back to the burnt-out trailer a few days later she had seen them, black and twisted and melted into odd shapes. The curtains had been in the living room. She didn't remember seeing them in flames like in the dream. The real fire was a blur, but the dream was so vivid.

Melissa pushed the indigo-light button on her watch and checked the time. 1:00 AM. She picked up her flashlight, got out of bed and went in search of a drink. She poured a glass of water from the plastic water jug and then turned off her flashlight. She could see perfectly in the moonlight streaming through the big front window.

Melissa stood at the window and gazed out. Sharlene was sitting in a lawn chair at the top of the grassy slope. She looked so still that Melissa wondered if she were asleep. She hesitated, then carried her glass of water outside, the porch door clicking softly behind her.

Sharlene turned her head and said, "Hello, twelve-year-old."

"Hi," said Melissa. She slid into the lawn chair beside Sharlene and pulled her knees up to her chest.

The sweat had dried on her back but her T-shirt felt clammy and there were goose bumps on her arms.

"Can't sleep?"

"No," said Melissa. She stared hard at a package of cigarettes, still in their cellophane wrapper, and a silver lighter resting on the arm of Sharlene's chair. "Are you going to smoke?" she blurted.

"I thought I was when I brought them outside," said Sharlene. "I was absolutely sure I was going to." She smiled at Melissa. "But no, I'm not."

"Is that because of the fire hazard?" said Melissa.

"No, I would've been careful. It's because I don't want to anymore."

A tiny knot in the back of Melissa's neck melted. "Where did you get them?" she said.

"I brought them from home. I was afraid I might need them."

"I don't suppose I could try one?" said Melissa. "Now that I'm almost a teenager."

"No, I don't suppose you could," said Sharlene firmly.

Melissa slid deeper into the chair. She didn't really want to smoke a cigarette; it looked like it would be disgusting. She just wanted to see what Sharlene would say. She examined the butterflies on her fingernails. They were pale and silvery in the moonlight.

"You were pretty quiet all evening," said Sharlene.
Melissa lifted her shoulders up and down.

"Anything happen today?"

"Sort of." Melissa swallowed. The memory of her
fear when she had thought that the fire on the island
was going to shoot into the trees was still raw. She
hadn't planned to tell Sharlene but the words spilled
out now in a rush.

"Alice and I made a fire on the island. I told her
I didn't want to, but she wanted to try cooking
bannock. The fire got way too big and the wind was
blowing the flames everywhere."

Sharlene didn't say anything but Melissa could tell
she was listening intently.

"I was so scared," whispered Melissa. Suddenly
tears started sliding down her cheeks and she felt her
entire body start to shake.

"Oh, honey, of course you were scared," said
Sharlene. "My god, it was an incredibly foolish thing
to do. But it's over and nothing happened. That's
what's important now."

Melissa wiped her cheeks. "You won't tell Ted, will
you?"

"No, I don't think Ted needs to know." Sharlene
frowned. "Alice seems to me like a very troubled girl."

"She's all right." Melissa pushed away her confusion
over Alice's lies. She took a big breath. "Mom, when the

trailer caught on fire…would I have seen the curtains burning?"

"What do you mean?" said Sharlene.

"It's always in the dream," said Melissa. "Flames are shooting up the curtains in the living room. But I don't remember seeing that."

"You wouldn't have," said Sharlene slowly. "At least I don't think so. You were in your bedroom when I found you. We got you and Cody out the bedroom window. But I saw the curtains burning. Maybe I talked about it and you heard me."

"I don't remember going back to my bedroom." Melissa could feel tears welling behind her eyes again. "I should have stayed in the kitchen and tried to put the fire out," she said miserably. "It was all my fault."

"You were nine years old," said Sharlene quietly. "You shouldn't have been alone in the kitchen in the first place, especially not with a big pot of cooking oil that I hadn't bothered to put away. That was *my* fault."

"But maybe I could have stopped it from spreading or something," Melissa persisted. "If I hadn't run away."

"Melissa," said Sharlene, "you were a little kid. You were in horrible pain and you were scared. I'm the one who screwed up. I'm the adult, and it's my job to keep you and Cody safe. And I didn't do that."

Melissa's chest tightened. "Why didn't you keep us safe?" she whispered.

Sharlene was silent for a long time. Then she said, "Darren and I had been drinking all afternoon. The truth is, we were passed out. That's why it took so long for me to hear you. That's what happened, Melissa, and I will never forgive myself."

"I wanted so badly to make French fries," said Melissa slowly. "It looked so easy when you did it. But I don't remember much after that."

The counselor had explained to Melissa what everyone figured had happened. Melissa had turned on the element under the pot of oil that Sharlene had been using to make French fries the day before. Maybe she had even turned it on high. Oil ignites when it gets too hot, the counselor had said. The flames must have shot up, burning Melissa's hand and setting the cupboards above the stove on fire. No one was sure what Melissa had done after that, but Sharlene had found her in her bedroom, screaming.

"When am I going to stop having the fire dream?" said Melissa.

"I don't know, Mel," said Sharlene softly. "But I do know that it will stop. One day."

Sharlene sounded so sure. Melissa shivered. She wasn't ready to go back to bed yet. "Do you think we could have some hot chocolate?"

"I think that's an excellent idea," said Sharlene. She stood up and stretched. "I'll make it, and you stay here and wrap this blanket around you."

The plaid blanket from the couch was draped over the back of Sharlene's chair. Melissa pulled it over her shoulders. She listened drowsily to the sounds drifting through the screened window as Sharlene heated up milk on the campstove.

How long had her mother been sitting here in the night, trying desperately not to smoke a cigarette? Had she even been to bed? Maybe she sat here every night after Melissa went to sleep.

Melissa's thoughts floated to Alice. She had been so furious when Melissa put out the fire. A shiver ran up Melissa's back when she remembered Alice's blazing eyes. Tomorrow was Friday, the day Melissa was supposed to jump off the cliff. It had been exactly one week since they made the pact. Would Alice remember? Would she even care? Melissa took a deep breath. None of that mattered anymore. She wasn't going back to Dar Wynd. Not ever. She sighed and huddled deeper into the warmth of the blanket. She felt safe now.

Eighteen

The next day, Melissa sunbathed after lunch. At three o'clock she went into the cabin for a cold drink. Cody and Sharlene were napping on their bunk beds. Melissa didn't know what she wanted to do with the rest of the afternoon. She felt a little bit sick. Alice must have figured out by now that she wasn't coming to the island.

Melissa went into her bedroom and dug out the wolf needlepoint kit from her box labeled *Melissa*. She propped herself up on her bed and scanned the instructions. She decided to start with the full moon in the corner of the tapestry. It turned out to be easy, the same slanted stitch with the creamy white wool over and over again, and you definitely couldn't call it *art*. It was more like paint by numbers. But it was something to do.

In the evening, Sharlene declared Melissa the winner of the Flycatcher Lake Boggle Tournament and suggested they move on to something else. Melissa sorted through the boxes of games. Some of them were missing pieces. There was one called Quest that she hesitated over. It had knights and castles and she thought that Alice would love it. Then she put it back on the shelf. She didn't plan on ever seeing Alice again. Melissa finally decided on Chinese Checkers, which delighted Sharlene, who said it was a classic and they had played it at her grandpa's cabin by the hour.

The next day, after breakfast, Sharlene declared that she needed a holiday from studying and took Cody fishing in the canoe. Unaccustomed to having the morning to herself, Melissa roamed around the cabin restlessly. Finally she settled in the shady porch and worked on the needlepoint. When the full moon was finished, Melissa stood up and stretched and went in search of cookies.

The cabin was cool, and Melissa decided to draw at the kitchen table. Just before noon she heard voices from outside on the dock, Cody's high-pitched excited chatter, Sharlene laughing at something and then a third voice. Alice.

Melissa froze, staring at her piece of paper. For a second she wondered wildly if she could flee to her bedroom, but then it was too late. They were all on the porch.

Cody had a fish, just big enough to keep and eat. It was silvery with a pale red stripe down its side. There was a flurry of confusion for a few minutes as Melissa dutifully examined the fish while Cody proudly swung it in her face. Melissa was conscious of Alice standing there quietly, watching.

"We agreed that we weren't coming in until we caught one," said Sharlene. "We ran out of snacks ages ago and I was beginning to worry about starvation."

Alice spoke up. "That's a trout. You can eat it. Austin catches them all the time."

"In that case," said Sharlene, "we'll put it in ice while I make lunch, and then we'll attempt to clean it. You'll have some lunch with us, Alice? It's just going to be peanut-butter-and-banana sandwiches."

Alice looked pleased. "Sure. Thanks."

"I'll help," said Melissa quickly, avoiding Alice's eyes. Alice drifted over to Cody's pile of toys and helped him load up his dump truck with blocks while Melissa spread peanut butter on bread. Alice *was* good with Cody. She chattered away to him. His voice got louder and louder with excitement but she didn't seem to mind.

Melissa tried to sort out her thoughts as she sliced up a couple of bananas. What was going on? Alice was acting as if that whole horrible thing with the fire had never happened.

They ate inside at the kitchen table. When they were finished, Sharlene took Cody to the outhouse.

"I wondered where you were yesterday," Alice said casually.

Melissa felt her cheeks redden. She swallowed her last bite of a chocolate-chip cookie and mumbled, "I was just really busy."

"You missed your jumping day. But of course you know that." Alice smiled at Melissa. "It doesn't really matter. Wednesday is your new jumping day. I'll probably jump again with you."

Alice ran her fingers through her cropped hair, making it stand out in a pale cloud around her thin face. "I've written the next part of my story. Mareea's left Elfrida at the pass above the spriggans' valley."

Wednesday, thought Melissa. She swallowed.

"The battle scene is going to be exciting." Alice's voice rose. "It's just Elfrida against all those spriggans so the sword will have to be magical or something."

Melissa didn't say anything. She tried to imagine what Alice would say when she told her she wasn't going to jump.

"Melissa, come back to Dar Wynd," said Alice suddenly.

Melissa stiffened.

"Please." Two blotches of red spread across Alice's cheeks. "I'm sorry I acted like such an idiot."

Before Melissa could think of a reply, Sharlene and Cody returned. Alice stood up. "Can I help clean up?" she said politely.

"Thanks, Alice, but no," said Sharlene. "There's nothing really to do. You girls go ahead."

"In that case, let's go to the island," said Alice.

"Me too!" shrieked Cody.

"You have a fish to clean, young man," said Sharlene.

"Are you coming, Melissa?" said Alice.

Melissa drained her glass of lemonade and slowly got up from the table. Alice had sounded really sorry. And besides, Melissa had missed being at Dar Wynd. "Okay," she said finally.

Alice said they could go in her canoe and she would bring Melissa back to the cabin. Melissa agreed, though secretly she wondered if Alice just wanted a chance to hang around her family again. Melissa pulled hard with her paddle and watched the water stream by in two silver lines on either side of the bow. She puzzled over how weird it was that Alice seemed to actually enjoy playing with Cody. And Alice acted like she didn't mind Sharlene at all. Melissa sighed. She was so used to bracing herself for being embarrassed by her mother that this was a strange feeling.

"Are you listening?" said Alice.

"What?" said Melissa over her shoulder.

"I was telling you about my story," said Alice crossly.

"Oh," said Melissa. She pulled her mind to Elfrida and Tristan. "So how is it going to end anyway? Is Elfrida going to save Tristan?"

"Of course," said Alice. A sharp edge in her voice took Melissa aback. "That's the whole point. Elfrida saves him and brings him back to her family. Elfrida—"

Alice's voice broke off as the flat rock came into sight. An aluminum boat with a motor was tied to the overhanging tree. "That's Austin's boat," she said.

Melissa felt an instant surge of disappointment. Austin must have finally finished haying and had come out to the island to hang around with Alice. Having a teenaged boy at Dar Wynd would change everything, no matter how great Alice said he was.

She was suddenly aware that Alice had stopped paddling. When she turned around she saw that Alice's eyes were wide with apprehension.

"What's wrong?" said Melissa.

Alice blinked hard. "Nothing's wrong. Why would anything be wrong? Sometimes, Melissa, you say strange things." She thrust her paddle back in the water and the canoe bumped up against the rock. Alice scrambled out. Melissa climbed out stiffly beside her.

"He must be at Dar Wynd," said Alice.

There was no doubt in Melissa's mind now. Alice sounded frightened. Melissa's head whirled with confusion. Why?

At that moment the sound of cracking sticks made both girls turn and stare at the path that led into the woods. A moment later, Austin strode through the trees. He was wearing cutoff jeans and a black T-shirt, and his long dark hair hung over his eyes. In one hand he carried the silver sword; with his other hand he clutched some books to his chest.

His face was twisted with anger. He stopped abruptly. "There you are," he said, his words stabbing the air. His eyes blazed with fury and a jolt of fear ran through Melissa. What was going on?

"What the hell are you doing with my stuff?" the boy spat. His words snapped like shards of ice. "Who do you think you are, just helping yourself to whatever you want?"

A chill ran up Melissa's spine. Beside her, Alice said, her voice barely louder than a whisper, "It wasn't like that. Honestly."

"Oh yeah? Then why are my books here? And my sword?"

"I was just borrowing them," said Alice. "I wasn't hurting anything."

"Is that what happened to my forty bucks too? You just *borrowed* it right off my dresser?"

Alice was silent. Melissa felt sick when she thought of the two twenty-dollar bills tucked into her birthday card.

Austin slid the books onto the floor of the aluminum boat and laid the sword against a seat. Then he stood up and said fiercely, "This sword is mine! Get it? Mine! Keep your hands off it. And what is that crap you're writing about Tristan?"

"You read my story?" gasped Alice.

"Yeah, I read it. It was lying right there. How dare you put Tristan in it! Don't you even care?"

"It's not really Tristan," said Alice. She sounded terrified now. "It's just a character I made up."

"Then you shouldn't have called him Tristan. You shouldn't have used his name. It's...*sick*. You make me sick."

"Austin, don't," pleaded Alice.

Austin stepped forward and gave her a rough shove. "Get out of my way. And don't ever touch my stuff again. You got it? Never!"

Austin jumped down into his boat. It rocked back and forth. He untied the rope and then knelt beside the motor and savagely yanked the cord. The motor sputtered and then roared to life.

He glared at Alice with cold eyes and shouted above the roar of the motor. "Dad says you're supposed to come home right now. We're going to town to get tractor parts and you have to stay with Mom."

"Please—"

"Do as I say! And shut up! Just shut up!"

Alice stood beside Melissa, frozen, until the boat had disappeared. Then she sank down on the flat rock and hugged her knees tightly.

Melissa felt like she was going to throw up. She took a big breath. Then she sat beside her friend and said softly, "Alice, who is Tristan?"

Nineteen

Alice didn't say anything.

Melissa repeated gently, "Tristan? Who is he?"

"You won't understand," said Alice.

"Yes, I will," said Melissa, although she wasn't entirely sure she would.

"My brother," whispered Alice.

"But…I thought it was just you and Austin…" Melissa's voice trailed off in confusion.

"My *little* brother," said Alice. "He died two years ago, just before we moved here. He was four."

The same age as Cody. Shock and horror filled Melissa. "What happened?" she said.

"He had cancer," said Alice. Her voice sounded

flat, drained of emotion. "He got sicker and sicker and then he just died."

Tears slid down Alice's cheeks. Melissa reached out and touched her arm. "I'm so sorry."

Alice swiped her eyes. "Austin thinks he misses Tristan more than I do. But he's wrong. I miss Tristan every day. Sometimes I hate Austin."

"But I thought...you said you guys did all that stuff together."

"I made it up," said Alice bitterly. "He *used* to like me. But now he doesn't even know I exist."

Melissa felt a pang of sorrow as she thought of the photograph she had found in Alice's leather book. Austin's arm was slung around Alice's shoulder, the little boy with the round tummy was tucked securely in front of them, and they had all been grinning. The little boy had a name now. Tristan. And he wasn't Alice's cousin. He was her brother.

An icicle ran up her back as she tried to imagine Cody dying of some horrible disease, and she knew in that instant how terribly she would miss him. She swallowed hard, trying to think of something to say, but her brain was frozen.

Alice stood up. She picked up a small rock from the ground and hurled it far out into the lake. "Austin can go to hell," she said. "They can all go to hell."

Then she was crying properly, her shoulders heaving with sobs.

"I'm so sorry," said Melissa again, feeling helpless. She had a sudden thought that her mother would know what to do and she wished that Sharlene were there.

Alice stopped crying. The tears left dirty streaks on her cheeks, and her nose was running. She sniffed hard and took several huge shaky breaths. She looked at Melissa. "You're so lucky," she said.

"Me?" said Melissa.

"You have such a perfect family."

"I don't," said Melissa quickly. "I really don't."

"I wish I had your mother," said Alice.

"But your mother is great. She has that important job." Melissa felt everything dissolve. "Sharlene didn't even graduate. She's a *custodian* in my school!"

"So?" said Alice. "Who cares? And I lied about my mother's job too."

Melissa stared at her. "You did?"

"She *used* to work for a publishing company. Before Tristan died. Now she doesn't do anything." Alice's voice was jagged. "She doesn't even get out of bed most days. She won't even let anyone open the curtains."

"What's the matter with her?" said Melissa, shocked.

"The doctor calls it depression," said Alice. "It's because of Tristan dying. She was fine before that."

"Why doesn't your father make her get up?" said Melissa.

"Dad ignores her," said Alice bitterly. "He spends all his time outside working. Everything changed when Tristan died. Dad used to be fun. Now I don't think he cares about any of us. He just yells about the house being dirty all the time. And if I'm late making dinner, then he gets really mad."

That was why Alice had looked panicky when she saw how late she had stayed at the birthday party. Melissa felt numb.

"Can't somebody do something?" Melissa hesitated. "A social worker or something?" She remembered a very sympathetic social worker who had visited them a few times after the fire. Melissa had pretended that the social worker was her mother.

Alice flushed. "We don't want a social worker poking around. It's nobody's business but ours. I shouldn't even have told you."

"I won't tell anyone," said Melissa quickly. "I promise."

"There's no point talking about any of this," Alice burst out. She hurled another rock.

Then she said, in a voice that sounded hollow and empty, "Austin said I had to go home. Mom must be having one of her really bad days. I better go right now."

In the late afternoon, clouds started piling up at the end of the lake, and by supper time they had blotted out the sun completely. A stiff breeze rattled the leaves in the aspen trees.

"I think it's actually going to rain," said Sharlene. "That's probably not a bad thing. The firefighters will be happy."

Melissa helped gather up the lawn-chair cushions and the towels draped over the backs of chairs and on the dock. She found herself worrying about Alice's stuff in the tree house. It would get ruined if it rained. She gazed out at the lake. The sky and the water were the same dark shade of gray and the air felt heavy.

"I have to go back to the island to do something," she told Sharlene. "I won't be long."

The first few drops of rain made dimples on the glassy lake as she paddled up to the flat rock. She ran along the trail to the tree house, scrambled up the ladder and pulled herself through the hole. Her heart gave a jolt. Scattered across the floor were scraps of paper covered in Alice's handwriting. She knew right away that it was Alice's story. She picked up a scrap and stared at it in horror. Austin did this, she thought shakily. He had been furious that Alice had put Tristan in the story. So furious that he had ripped it to pieces.

Slowly Melissa gathered up all the pieces. Uncertain what to do with them, she put them on the shelf and then looked around. For a moment she wished she hadn't come. Most of the stuff would be okay in the rain—the dishes, the cans of food, the bow and arrows. Austin had taken all the books. She rolled up the sleeping bag and stuffed it in a plastic garbage bag. She hesitated for a moment and then slid all the pieces of Alice's story into the front of the red binder. A paper was sticking out at the back. Melissa slipped it out and studied it for a moment. It was her drawing of Elfrida. The young girl's face looked proud and brave. Melissa remembered Alice saying excitedly, "It looks like me!" She kept the picture aside to take back with her and slid the binder into the top of the garbage bag.

Melissa tied the flaps at the top of the bag and slid it under the shelf. She took one last look around. When Melissa had first seen the tree house, a tingle had run up her spine as if she really were in a magical place. But now she just felt tired, and Dar Wynd seemed like a game she had played a long time ago.

The rain was falling harder now and a chill crept over Melissa. She tucked the drawing under her shirt to keep it dry. As she made her way back along the darkening trail to her canoe, she shivered at the memory of Austin's fury. She wondered if Dar Wynd would ever feel magical again.

Twenty

S harlene had decided to save Cody's fish for breakfast and she made hamburgers for supper. Melissa put together a salad while Sharlene fried the burgers on the campstove.

Supper smelled good, but when it came time to eat, Melissa found it hard to swallow. She played with her food and ended up dumping most of it in the garbage. For the rest of the evening she was torn between telling Sharlene what had happened and keeping her promise to Alice. She caught Sharlene looking at her searchingly a few times, but her mother didn't ask and Melissa kept quiet.

The rain had turned into a steady downpour and sent everyone to bed early. Melissa lay on her back with her window open, listening to the rain pattering on the roof.

What was Alice doing right now? Austin had ordered Alice to come home to stay with their mother because she was having a bad day. What did that mean? Melissa had a vague picture in her mind of a woman with a sad face lying in a bed in a dark bedroom, the curtains pulled tight. She remembered times when Sharlene had stayed in bed all day, hungover from a party. Melissa had crept around the trailer, trying to keep Cody from making too much noise, preparing meals of tinned spaghetti and crackers. But Sharlene had always gotten up eventually and she had never seemed depressed.

All that felt like a long time ago now, and Melissa realized with surprise that she didn't think about it that much anymore. Through the thin walls she heard Cody call out something in a distressed voice and she instinctively tensed, ready to go to him. Then came the reassuring murmur of Sharlene's voice, soft and comforting. Melissa waited a moment and then rolled over on her side and drifted into a deep, exhausted sleep.

It rained on and off for the next two days. Each afternoon a watery sun came out for a couple of hours and Melissa went back to Dar Wynd. Everything was exactly as she had left it. There was no sign of Alice. Melissa's stomach clenched at the thought that something bad had happened, something awful enough to keep Alice away.

After supper on the second day, while Sharlene went to the store, Melissa helped Cody build a castle out of toilet-paper rolls, old yogurt containers and his blocks. "We'll call it Dar Wynd," she said when it was finished. Cody had been filling the courtyard with his plastic animals but he looked up at Melissa and said, "What's Dar Wynd?"

"It's a very special place," said Melissa. "But I'm going to let you borrow the name."

Sharlene came in with a bag of groceries. She admired the castle and then Melissa got Cody ready for bed. She read him three stories and then came back into the main room. Sharlene was standing by the window, staring outside. She turned around and said, "I heard some very shocking news from Marge at the store. I didn't want to tell you in front of Cody."

"What is it?" said Melissa. Her chest tightened. Sharlene had hardly said anything since she got back from the store and now she looked upset. What could have happened?

Sharlene sank onto one end of the couch, and Melissa stared at her. "What is it?" she said again.

"It's Alice's mother," said Sharlene. "Apparently she's been very ill. Mentally ill. No one in the community knew. And the night before last..." Sharlene's voice trailed off.

"What happened?" said Melissa.

"She took a whole bunch of pills," said Sharlene.

An icy chill sank deep into Melissa's stomach. "What kind of pills?"

"I don't know," said Sharlene. "Sleeping pills, maybe. Alice found her, which is awful. It turns out they don't even have a phone down there. Alice's father rushed her to the store, and Marge phoned an ambulance but he was afraid to wait for it. It's two hours to the nearest hospital. Alice's father raced down the highway and met the ambulance on the way. It's a wonder he didn't have an accident. He must have been so frantic."

Melissa sat down on the couch beside Sharlene. "Is she going to be all right?" she said. Her mouth felt dry.

"She survived the pills," said Sharlene. "They must have pumped out her stomach. But Marge says they'll be keeping her in the hospital for quite a while." Sharlene sighed. "Here she was, this poor woman, a neighbor, and no one had any idea she was so unhappy."

"I knew," whispered Melissa. "Alice told me. The last time I saw her. Alice had a little brother called Tristan. He died two years ago of cancer when he was four, and her mother has been like this ever since. Tristan was in Alice's story."

Sharlene squeezed Melissa's hand. "Oh, honey. How sad. No wonder Alice was so drawn to Cody."

"You'd think it would just make her feel bad being around him," said Melissa. "He would remind her of Tristan."

"Alice wouldn't need any reminding," said Sharlene gently. "And everyone is different. I think Cody helped Alice escape. In an odd way he might have brought Tristan back."

A miserable feeling of guilt welled up in Melissa. "If I had told you about her mother, do you think we could have done something?"

"No, I don't," said Sharlene. "And you mustn't start thinking like that. Melissa, in the big picture this may not be a bad thing. Maybe now Alice's mother will get the help she needs."

"Alice and Austin need help too," said Melissa.

Sharlene nodded. "And now they have a chance. Families can mend, you know."

Melissa thought about that for a moment. She thought about a family breaking apart, like a piece of china, and then being stuck back together again.

"Alice lied to me about so many things," she said with a sigh. "She said she and Austin built the tree house and that he was this great brother, but he wasn't. He acts like he hates Alice! And it was Alice who stole the stuff from our cabin. She said the window was already broken but I'm not even sure now if that's true. She probably broke it herself."

"I suspected it was Alice," said Sharlene slowly.

"She was supposed to be my friend," said Melissa. "Friends don't lie to each other."

"She was the best friend she could be at this time in her life," said Sharlene firmly. "Just think, Mel, how Alice must have felt when her little brother died. Helpless. I think all those crazy things she did and even her lying, was her way of trying to have some control over her life."

"What will happen to Alice now?" said Melissa.

"Marge said that Alice's aunt has arrived from Toronto," said Sharlene. "She stopped in at the store and Marge said she seemed extremely sensible and kind. Austin and Alice are going to move to Toronto and live with her for a while." Sharlene stood up. "I have a feeling Alice is a survivor. She'll be okay."

The next day Alice's aunt brought Alice over to say goodbye. Her aunt, a tall freckled woman called Penny, who reminded Melissa of Jill Templeton, drank iced tea with Sharlene on the porch. Melissa and Alice sat on the end of the dock, dangling their legs in the water.

"I'm almost all packed," said Alice. "Austin just started packing this morning. He said he wasn't going to go at first, but he's changed his mind. Aunty Penny says he can sign up for hockey. Austin used to be really good at hockey, before Tristan died. I get to pick something to do too. I can do swimming or skating or whatever I want." Alice's thin face glowed. "I might pick dance."

A survivor, thought Melissa. Sharlene was right. "I went back to Dar Wynd," she said. "I put the sleeping bag in a garbage bag so it wouldn't get wet."

"Oh, thanks," said Alice, but she sounded uninterested. Then she frowned. "Did you find my story? Did Austin really rip it up? That's what he told me."

Melissa nodded. "I picked up all the pieces. They're in the binder. I put that in the garbage bag too. You might be able to put the story together."

Alice shrugged. "It was dumb anyway. And I probably never would have finished it. Oh, and by the way," she added airily, "you can have Dar Wynd if you want."

Melissa stiffened. Dar Wynd wasn't Alice's to give away. She sighed. She didn't think she would want to hang out there by herself anyway. One day, when she felt like it, she would go back to Dar Wynd and gather up all the stuff Alice had taken and bring it back to the cabin.

Alice made a face. "When I go to Toronto, I have to go back into grade six. That's because I haven't actually done any schoolwork for over a year. But Aunt Penny says her neighbor has a daughter who will be in my class. We're going to invite her over as soon as I get there."

Melissa stretched her legs out and watched the water drip off her toes. She imagined Alice peppering this girl with questions. Alice had said that Melissa was her best friend, but she didn't seem at all sad about leaving her. Melissa tried to sort out her jumbled feelings. She thought she should feel a little bit jealous, but to her surprise she didn't. She wondered what grade seven was going to be like. There had been a new girl in her class the last month of school who Melissa had thought seemed nice. She made a plan to summon the nerve to ask her over.

When it was time to go, Sharlene gave Alice a big hug. Then Alice hugged Melissa.

"Wait a minute," said Melissa. She ran into the cabin and got the two twenty-dollar bills off her dresser. The drawing of Elfrida that she had thumbtacked on the wall caught her eye. It was the only thing she had to remind her of Alice, but she didn't really need it. She would *never* forget Alice.

Melissa hesitated and then took it down. She went outside and gave the money to Alice. "You better give this back to Austin. And here's your picture."

Alice took the money quickly and put it in her pocket. She studied the drawing of Elfrida, her face unreadable. "She would have done it, you know. She would have saved Tristan."

"I know," said Melissa.

Alice folded the picture carefully. "I'll keep this forever," she said.

She climbed into the passenger seat of her aunt's red car and rolled down the window. "Goodbye, goodbye," she called.

Aunt Penny turned her car around and, beeping the horn, bounced up the rutted road. The last thing Melissa saw was Alice's arm waving wildly out the window.

Twenty-One

"Mom!" called Melissa. "Cody did it! He put his face in the water!"

Sharlene put her book down on the arm of the lawn chair. She stood up to get a better look. "Let me see!" she said.

"Come on, Cody, you can do it one more time," urged Melissa.

Cody scrunched up his cheeks. He took a big breath. He leaned over from his waist and dipped his face in the water. He threw his head back up in a shower of sunlit water drops, sputtering and gasping.

"Bravo!" shouted Sharlene. "Way to go! And kudos to the instructor."

Melissa grinned. She surveyed her little brother, slippery and wet as a minnow, and said, "Now I'm going to teach you how to do a dead man's float."

❦

It was Melissa's day to jump.

She stood on the smooth sun-warmed rock at the top of the cliff and gazed down into the still, green bay. Dark shadows clung along the base of the cliff, but farther out the water sparkled in the sun.

The cliff was higher than she remembered. Melissa's knees felt weak.

She bit her lip. "One, two, three," she said softly.

She braced her back and willed herself to go but her legs felt stuck to the ground.

For a second, Melissa closed her eyes. Far out in the lake a loon warbled.

You'll love it, Alice had promised. *You'll feel free like an eagle.*

Melissa opened her eyes. "One, two three..." She sucked in a huge gulp of air and leaped off the cliff.

She felt a whoosh of air on her arms and face. Everything spun around her in a blur of green and blue. Then she hit the water with a great splash.

She sank down, down—much deeper than she had expected. She was lost in a cool, dim green world and she felt a moment of panic. Her chest was going to explode. Then she turned her head up to the light and swam with steady strokes, feeling the strength in her arms from days of paddling.

She burst out into a blaze of blinding sun and blue water.

She gasped, feeling the air pour into her lungs. "Whooo-eeee!" she hollered. "I did it!"

Melissa took her time paddling back to the cabin, the warm sun seeping into her shoulders and back. That morning, Sharlene had asked her if she wanted to go back to Huntley. "We've got two weeks left until school starts," she said. "We don't have to stay here if you don't want to. We can move into our new place a bit early, I'm sure."

Melissa thought about the new apartment. She couldn't wait to move in. But there was still so much she wanted to do at the lake. "I want to stay," she said.

Two weeks. She dug her paddle deeper and made her plans. Bonnie Hill had invited them to the guest ranch to go horseback riding. Melissa had never been on a horse but she was pretty sure she could do it. And there was the fair. She had decided that she would enter some of her drawings. And Sharlene had predicted that Cody would be floating any day now.

Ted had dropped by in the morning and told them that the fire ban was lifted. He was coming for supper and Sharlene had promised that they could roast hot dogs on a campfire and make something called s'mores out of graham crackers, chocolate and marshmallows. Sharlene said s'mores were one of the best things about summers at her grandpa's cabin.

Melissa's stomach rumbled as she paddled past the island. Their cabin came into view. Sharlene was reading in a lawn chair and Cody was playing in the grass with his dump truck. Melissa rested the paddle for a moment and waved.

Sharlene had talked about their new life. Melissa had waited and waited for it. Now she knew it had crept up on her without her knowing. She grinned as she dug her paddle into the smooth water and felt the canoe surge forward.

Acknowledgments

A huge thank-you to my writing pals, Kathy, Ann and Ainslie, who make writing fun, and to my sister Janet, who reads all my manuscripts. As well, a heartfelt thanks to my editor Sarah Harvey, who brings out the best in my writing.

BECKY CITRA is the author of many books for children, including *Never to be Told*, *Whiteout* and the Max and Ellie historical series. Becky lives on a ranch in Bridge Lake, British Columbia, where she cross-country skis, rides her horses and watches the wildlife that visits her home.